THE

SECRET ROAD
HOME

THE
SECRET ROAD

HOME

ROBERT L. WISE

BROADMAN
& HOLMAN
PUBLISHERS

Nashville, Tennessee

13-digit ISBN: 978-0-8054-3074-5
10-digit ISBN: 0-8054-3074-1

Published by Broadman & Holman Publishers,
Nashville, Tennessee

Dewey Decimal Classification: F
Subject Headings: ESCAPES—FICTION
                    WORLD WAR, 1939–45—
                       CAUSES—FICTION
                    HOLOCAUST, 1933–45—FICTION

06 07 08 09 10   10 9 8 7 6 5 4 3 2 1

ACKNOWLEDGMENTS

Supportive and helpful friends are a gift. My deepest appreciation to Bettie Beck, Bernice McShane, Dorothy Richardson, Rhonda Whittacre, and my son Matthew Tate Wise for their thoughts, suggestions, and responses while the manuscript was being prepared. George R. Simmons, a pilot in WWII who flew P-47s and was a prisoner of war in Stalag Luft 1, North III Compound, also gave insight and inspiration for the story. Your help put the frosting on the cake.

While fiction, this story is based on the brave work of the family of Julien and Ann Brusselman and their children Yvonne and Jacques. After the war ended, the Belgium, British, and American governments recognized this family's services with honors. Yes, there really is a 127 Rue d'Ixelles in Brussels where these events occurred.

PART ONE

The Year of Crisis—
1943

PROLOGUE

October 25, 2004

Jack Martin shook the newspaper uneasily. The column was short, but it was still a memoir on the war and that bothered him. Jack didn't like any story about *that* war. Even thinking of World War II made him nervous, edgy, and silent. Of course the war was ages ago, but the memories never stopped bothering him. He turned the page quickly, and started searching through the movie advertisements.

Though a tall man who stayed unusually fit, Jack's eighty-one years had still taken its toll, leaving deep lines under his brown eyes and around his narrow mouth. A double chin hung from his neck, but he still looked fairly well.

Off in the other room the telephone rang, but Martha would answer it. During the decades since their children George and Mary left home, his wife made it her habit *always* to answer the phone first. The irresistible impulse seemed like some sort of mania with Mary. Jack listened but could only hear her mumbling something or other.

Jack didn't like to admit that his hearing wasn't what it once was. He buried his head in the newspaper again. The sports section declared that the University of Oklahoma might again have the number one football team in the country. Bad news for Texas fans.

The weather report said an unexpected cold wind was coming down the plains and would sweep over Dallas and the rest of Texas, leaving more than a hint of autumn in the air. Leaves already had started to fall and the evening air felt brisk, but this time of the year always stimulated Jack Martin.

"Jack!" Martha called from the dining room. "You've got the strangest phone call." His gray-haired wife walked into the living room and pointed over her shoulder. "Some man says he is calling from a town called Maastrich. I think he said Maastrich, Germany."

Jack jerked as if Martha had shocked him with an electric wire. His mouth dropped, and he stared at his wife as if he'd seen a ghost. "I don't think I heard you right."

"Maastrich, dear. Some town in Europe."

Jack blinked several times, and wiped his mouth nervously. "*It can't be!*"

"Heavens! All I know is that some man with an accent says he's looking for a Jack Martin." Martha shrugged and rolled her eyes. "You know anyone in Germany of all places?"

Jack stared at his wife. "It can't be," he said and leaped out of his chair, stomping toward the dining room. "Just can't be."

"Can't be what?" Martha frowned.

Without answering her, Jack hurried to the phone and picked it up nervously. "Hello. This is Jack Martin."

"Ah! *Herr* Martin!" The clear, crisp voice sounded like the man was in the next room. "I am calling from Germany to see if you were the pilot of a United States B-17 Flying Fortress shot down during World War II."

"*World War II!*"

"*Ya,*" the caller spoke with an obvious German accent. "My name is Reinhold Schroder. I am part of a group that digs up objects left behind from the great war. I think your word for our efforts might be a 'hobby.' Recently, we found a piece of the fuselage of a B-17 Flying Fortress with a number and the words the *Flying Tiger* still painted boldly on this section. Does that awaken any memories?"

Jack Martin nearly choked. He had refused to mention the name *Flying Tiger* for more than five decades. He had to catch his breath.

"You are still there?"

"Sorry. Yes, yes. I was the pilot of that airplane just before it crashed."

"Ah! Excellent! Our records are correct! Most helpful. We are not clear, but it seems you would have had in your crew a navigator, turret gunner, a lead bombardier, perhaps a couple of other men."

Jack blinked several times. "Yes."

"Wonderful! Our members will be most excited. You see, we were all born after the war but grew up hearing about the conflict. Most exciting!"

"Yeah," Jack growled. "More than a little stimulating."

"What? I don't think I understand."

"That was a long time ago." Jack rubbed his forehead. "Way back there in the dusty past."

"*Ya.* Most certainly was," Reinhold Schroder said. "We are digging up the airplane to put the pieces in a museum in our city. I am calling to see if you have any pictures of yourself when you were the pilot. Maybe, a picture of you today?"

"Pictures?" Jack stirred uncomfortably. "I ... I ... don't know." He scratched his thinning gray hair. "I'd have to search."

"Most excellent! Our desire would be to call you back in a few weeks and see what you have found."

"You said your name was Schroder?"

"Reinhold Schroder. May I call you in, say, three weeks?"

"Three weeks?" Jack took another deep breath.

"Yes, and we'd be delighted to have any stories, memories, you'd like to share of what happened to you."

"Stories?" Jack started blinking again. "Huh! I don't know. I'll have to think about it some."

"Certainly. And if any other members of the *Flying Tiger* can be located, we'd like to communicate with them."

"I'll have to think about that too," Jack said slowly. "It'll take me some time."

"Of course, *Herr* Martin. I will be back in touch. *Dunken ja!*"
He hung up.

Jack slowly returned the receiver to the cradle and silently stared at the wall, trying to order his thoughts.

"Jack!" Martha marched in. "Your face doesn't look right. You appear white. Are you all right?"

Martin stood up haltingly, but didn't answer his wife's question. "I need to go outside and get some air."

"Air? Jack! It's getting cold. Are you okay?"

He didn't say anything but walked toward the back door, letting the screen slam behind him. Jack walked straight for the back fence and an empty corner where no one would interrupt him, certainly not Martha. The huge bright moon threw shadows across the back yard, but the gentle breeze felt more like a skin bracer. He inhaled deeply.

Far overhead the harvest moon looked round and clear, but the far off globe reminded Jack he was now eighty-one years old. More than occasionally the scars on his legs got tight, and the dark red blots could sting when the weather turned cold. The indentations where the flesh had been removed had stayed for decades. When the pain periodically came back, Jack had to grit his teeth but never, never did he mention the problem. Jack still had other aches and pains left over from the war, but for the last six decades he'd kept his mind off the disaster that had created the injuries. Not once had he told Martha or the children anything about that deadly airplane crash outside of Maastrich.

It was so long ago; it seemed like yesterday morning.

During the decades following the war, Jack had moved to Dallas and started his own insurance business. As the city grew, his business developed. Life had been extremely good to the Martin family. After their marriage he and Martha joined a church down the street and had been there virtually ever since. Eventually the children went down to Austin, and George and Mary graduated from the University of Texas. The Martins lived normal happy lives like most Americans. In time his hair grayed, and then after a decade of worry the thick brush thinned, but Jack never talked about the war.

The wind picked up, and Jack rubbed his arms. He wasn't good at talking with anyone about the past because what followed the crash of the *Flying Tiger* had so shaken him that Jack couldn't discuss the experience with anyone without becoming emotional. During the early years in the late forties and the fifties, he refused to even let himself think about it.

A tomcat abruptly jumped up on the fence and ran across the palings before disappearing into the alley. He watched the old cat disappear into the night and wanted to follow him.

Could he tell Martha . . . and George . . . and Mary . . . about those horrific experiences that so nearly cost him his life and had cost others theirs? Jack didn't think so. He didn't know if he could change his habit of silence or if he should even try. But the phone call no longer allowed him to push the memories aside. The past had come back for a visit and wouldn't be ignored.

The year was 1943 . . . sixty-one years ago.

CHAPTER ONE

September 2, 1943

The steady roar of the propellers echoed in Jack Martin's ears. With their mission over Berlin completed, the squadron of American bombers started their return to England. The constant noise of the B-17 Flying Fortress diminished the possibility of much lengthy personal conversation inside the body of the bomber, but Captain Jack Martin's crew had relaxed on their return from their five hundred-mile foray deep into Germany. Their flying formation had given the Berliners a run for their lives and most of the bombers escaped the massive *ack-ack* ground fire. Martin wasn't sure how many of their formation had gone down, but it was clear that any loss was not good. Nevertheless, all in all the flight had been a successful early morning run.

The entire formation kept their radios off to avoid tipping off the *Luftwaffe* as to which direction they might take in escaping. Unfortunately, Martin's airplane was bringing up the rear of the mission and that made them vulnerable. Usually navigators weren't used on these shorter runs, but because the *Flying Tiger* brought up the rear, this position had been covered in case of unexpected problems. One fact was sure. The Germans wouldn't let up.

Nazi persistence made sense to Captain Jack Martin. He had come from a German family background. His grandfather had immigrated to America with the name Heinrich Matthys. The old man quickly saw the need to "Americanize" himself and changed his last name to a more English sounding "Martin." Growing up around old Hennie Martin had taught Jack enough German that he understood the language and could speak it. He always felt more comfortable on these flights knowing it was possible to understand the enemy if anything turned out wrong.

With the formation cruising along at an altitude of 25,000 feet and with their oxygen masks in place, Jack started to breathe easier once they crossed the Rhine River and the Belgium border was in sight. A tall, thin officer with thick black hair, Martin had studied previous warfare in the area and knew how important the terrain underneath him had been in both World War I and during this struggle.

Martin's B-17 wasn't flying far from the Ardennes Forest, which had been regarded as impassable in World War I, but in this conflict the German Army Group A had made a surprise attack through the unprotected Ardennes, cutting the Allied forces in half in May 1940. Nazi paratroopers dropped immediately into the heart of Holland. At the same moment the Nazis struck in Belgium. With a minimal eighty-man force that had rehearsed on a mockup of the fort, they descended in gliders with *blitzkrieg* tactics at full tilt. A day later the Belgian fort of Eben-Emael fell to the Germans, opening the Albert Canal to use by Nazi troops flooding into Belgium. In three more days Rotterdam had been heavily bombed and Holland immediately surrendered. German Army Group A surged through the Ardennes and quickly pushed the French resistance out of their way. Hermann Goering's *Luftwaffe* then destroyed any trapped forces with air attacks.

King Leopold III surrendered the Belgian Army on May 28, 1940, without warning his allies. The Allied flank was suddenly fatally exposed, allowing German tanks, or panzers, to push toward the Channel. The surviving Allied forces had to retreat to the port of Dunkirk and run for their lives. Captain Martin certainly didn't want any similar problems with the *Luftwaffe* today.

"Captain, sir!" Lieutenant Hank Holt said over the microphone, "at our present speed we'll be coming up on Maastrich, Germany, in a couple of minutes. We're about on the Belgian border. So good so far, but we're far from out of the hands of the Jerries," the navigator observed.

"Keep me posted, Lieutenant," Martin answered. "Maastrich is an important area because it's close to Eben-Emael Fort and the Albert Canal. I'm sure the Germans will have plenty of antiair artillery waiting for us if we're identified."

"You got it, kid!" Holt answered and clicked off.

Jack especially liked Hank Holt because the small, stout man always kept his sense of humor no matter how complicated their problems became. If anybody was dependable, it was good old Hank.

Actually the entire crew of the *Flying Tiger* had proved to be good airmen. Martin's copilot, Al Smith, and the lead bombardier, Denver Meachem, had grown up together in Oklahoma and stayed buddies. Martin trusted their judgment, as well as that of his turret gunner Pat Taylor. Jake Gates had already proved himself a most capable tail gunner. Good men and more than trustworthy.

Martin particularly liked flying a B-17. The basics of flying the aircraft had been easy to learn, and the plane was always dependable. Flying Fortresses were not easy to knock down and stood up under considerable damage. If he had his choice, Captain Martin would choose to fly a Flying Fortress bomber any day of the week.

Jack heard an extra loud noise and looked up. From out of nowhere a Messerschmitt Bf 109E fighter roared out of the clouds, diving straight for their B-17. The piercing sound of machine gun fire ripped through the fuselage before the captain could even move. Instantly the glass in the cockpit shattered and Jack ducked his head, hanging on to the controls to keep the airplane stable.

"They hit us!" Hank Holt shouted into his microphone. "But I don't think they hit any engines."

"Hang on!" Martin shouted back. "The Krauts will be back!"

"Smith!" Martin said to his copilot sitting next to him. "Get a firm grip. We're in a bind. The Jerries are onto us."

No response.

Gripping the wheel even more tightly, Martin glanced at the copilot. Al Smith sat slumped against the side of the cockpit. Machine gun fire had caught him behind the neck, exploding a bullet through his chest and killing him.

Captain Martin gasped in terror. Blood was rushing down Smith's chest, over the seat, and splattering against the window. Al's arms hung limp at his side.

"God, help us!" Jack shouted into the mike. "They hit our copilot!"

"And they got our bombardier," some voice from the back reported. "Meacham's dead."

"Hang on!" Martin ordered. "Back there in the turret, make sure you're alert, Taylor. You too, Gates! That Messerschmitt will be back."

"Sir," Holt reported, "we're just about to come up on Maastrich. It's a good-sized town. Got to be heavily protected."

Jack grabbed the controls with a steel grip. The bomber couldn't be in a worse position than to be at the tail end of the formation with a Messerschmitt above them and antiartillery fire below them. The Germans certainly knew what to do to blow them out of the sky.

"Oh no!" Taylor the turret gunner bellowed into the intercom. "We're picking up a new Nazi attack plane. Another 109 is coming up at us from below."

Captain Martin turned on the radio to send the rest of the formation or any Allied fighter planes out there a message that they were in trouble. "Mayday! Mayday! This is Flying Fortress the *Flying Tiger*. Jerries are all over us. We're just about over Maastrich. Can we get any help?"

Martin waited for a reply but none came. If anyone in the formation had picked him up, no one was breaking the silence.

Artillery fire opened up from the ground and then suddenly the two Messerschmitts reappeared. One came from above and the other from beneath them, attacking only seconds apart. The B-17 rocked and shook while German machine gun fire strafed across the entire aircraft. Ground artillery burst through the wings, and instantly fire exploded from an engine on the left wing.

"We're hit!" the captain yelled into his microphone. "The left engine's gone. Prepare to jump. I don't think we can pull out." The airplane started downward into a dive. Flames leaped from the wings and smoke came rushing through the cockpit.

Jack took a deep breath. "God, help us," he prayed under his breath. "We're going down."

With no time to reflect, Captain Martin only reacted. Fire erupted around him, smoke rolled in the doorway and clouded the cracked windows around the fuselage. With one last yank on the wheel, he tried to pull the Flying Fortress out of the dive only to discover there was nothing he could do to level the airplane. Deterioration had already become too severe, and he could not reverse the downward drag. Hank Holt had already left the cockpit. Flipping off his safety harness, Jack struggled to climb out of the cockpit and get back to the side door to jump. Time was running out.

The body of the B-17 had already burst into flames, indicating that the Messerschmitts and the *ack-ack* ground fire had torn into the aircraft's fuel lines, possibly even igniting some of the ammunition. Smoke flowed through the airplane, making it difficult to see anything. Obviously, they were in more than serious trouble.

Martin could see men running through the smoke, heading to the door to jump. It was pointless to try to count the number of men escaping. Already too many of the crew had been killed.

At the tail end of the B-17 something exploded, knocking Martin backward against the bulkhead wall and sending a ball of fire roaring forward that instantly turned into a burst of black smoke. For a second Martin was stunned and unable to hear anything, then his stupor vanished as waves of fire shot up his legs. He looked down in horror to discover flames consuming his flight pants.

"Help!" Martin shouted, beating against his legs to put out the flames. "I'm on fire!"

In the roar of the fire spreading rapidly through their airplane plus the additional sound of wind swirling into the bomber, his voice went nowhere. The horrible agonizing pain of burning in his lower legs made Martin beat frantically on his pants, but the fire continued. Something flammable must have splashed on him.

"Get out!" Lieutenant Hank Holt's voice cut through the mayhem. "Everybody out!"

"Help me, Hank!" Jack screamed. "I'm burning up!"

Hank Holt rushed through the smoke. "You *are* on fire!" He grabbed a fire extinguisher and started spraying the flames. "We've got to get you out of here."

The throbbing pain had become nearly paralyzing. Captain Martin tried to stagger forward. Hank slipped his shoulder under Martin's armpit and pulled him toward the door.

"Forget that stuff about being the last man out!" Hank yelled. "I'm going to push you through the door, and jump out behind you. Get out of here before the entire airplane explodes."

Jack gritted his teeth. The pain in his legs remained too great to do anything more than nod his head. For a moment Martin was certain he would faint.

Lieutenant Holt kept beating on the flames and knocking out the fire, but the damage to his legs had already been done.

"Just get through that door and pull your rip chord," Holt instructed. "Can you do that?"

"Yeah," Martin groaned. "I think I can."

"I'll be behind you."

The captain could feel Hank pushing him toward the door. The B-17 went into an even sharper decline and flames shot higher. With a hard push, Holt hurled Jack through the door.

Jack tumbled head over heels, the fierce wind sending his body into a swirling spin toward the ground. The throbbing ache eased momentarily in the rush of the plunge toward the earth. The roar of the bomber's engines disappeared in this world of no sound. Jack had no sense of falling, only floating leisurely through the air like a leaf dropping gently to the ground. An ultimate sense of aloneness surrounded his idle, gentle descent to the earth. The sensation felt like he could float for days. With the return of the burning and throbbing in his legs, the illusion vanished.

Because he had no idea of his altitude, Jack recognized his dilemma. If he was too high and pulled the cord, there might not be enough oxygen and he could pass out. On the other hand, if he was too close to the ground, he could still come down with far too great an impact. The latter alternative seemed riskier so Jack released the parachute by yanking the D-ring on his side. When the parachute released, the harnesses shot up past him and he grabbed them. Jack fiercely held to the long nylon belts and prayed.

"God, help me out," Jack mumbled as the parachute tumbled out of the pack. "Oh, please. I don't want to die today!"

CHAPTER TWO

The telephone rang with a shrill buzz in the clandestine Gestapo office in Maastrich, Germany. The secretary instantly picked up the phone on the restricted line before referring the call to the area chief of operations.

A heavyset man, Arnwolf Mandel stared at the telephone for a moment. Why would anyone call him on his private line? He had not been expecting any outside calls this morning.

With an unusually round face and a neck that spilled over his collar, Mandel had the beady-blue eyes and thin nose that gave him the Aryan appearance that could only help his career. With blond hair plastered straight back on his head, Mandel tried to emulate SS boss Reinhard Heydrich's appearance as an additional boost for his career. Ironically, he and Heydrich had eyes with a striking similarity. The truth was Mandel's family background was Russian, but he ran from this fact like a retreat from death itself.

The telephone rang again.

"*Heil* Hitler! SS Officer Arnwolf Mandel speaking."

"*Heil* Hitler!" a man answered at once. "This is Colonel Bern Schmidt. I am with the *Wehrmacht*, Army Group B, Sixth Army. We have just received the report of an American B-17 bomber being shot down. Some of the crew were detected bailing out over your area. It is important to locate these men."

For a moment Arnwolf Mandel paused. Normally the Army had absolutely nothing to do with the Gestapo. In fact, the *Wehrmacht* retreated from *any* cooperation. Why would someone like Colonel Schmidt be calling his office for help?

"Excuse me," Mandel answered. "We usually do not receive calls for assistance from the Army. The Gestapo is a rather separate arm of *Der Führer*. I am somewhat surprised you would be seeking our help."

"I understand," Schmidt said in a professional voice. "At this time we are having problems catching these fleeing Allied invaders. We have a common interest in this geographic part of Belgium and must apprehend fleeing invaders before they cause problems for the Reich. I believe the group in question are Americans."

"I see," Arnwolf said slowly. "Interesting. Is this coming as an order?" He glanced across the room and momentarily studied his reflection in the mirror. "An edict?"

"Let me explain this unusual request," Schmidt continued.

Arnwolf listened, but his mind was elsewhere. No matter what the *Wehrmacht* said or wanted, this was an ideal situation for him. Arnwolf Mandel had only one fundamental interest—*self-promotion!* Ambition motivated the SS officer from the crack of dawn to the setting of the sun. Chasing down escaping Allied troopers fit his agenda perfectly. Most of his assignments were little more than routine investigations. Pursuing fleeing Allied soldiers had the possibility of shooting. Perhaps, one of these American dogs would be killed. Even better!

"Therefore," Schmidt concluded, "we would appreciate your assistance in this matter."

"At once!" Arnwolf answered. "I will be onto this matter personally before these American intruders even hit the ground! My car can take me to the crash area immediately. I will join your troops in scouring the area until we have rounded up all the swine. *Heil* Hitler!"

————————

The wind whipped furiously, shaking Captain Jack Martin back and forth during his slow descent onto the Belgium farm plain. Smoke continued to rise from his charred flight suit, and the burns stung intensely. Hanging tightly to the straps on his parachute, Jack had no alternative but to grit his teeth and allow the parachute to descend at its own rate of speed. Beneath him the Sambre Meuse River wound toward the Ardenne Forest, and off in the distance the town of Maastrich wasn't far to the north. Fearing he might pass out, Jack let his head drop while the parachute gently settled.

As the ground came closer, Captain Martin realized he must take control of the landing even if the pain in his legs overwhelmed him. Strong wind currents had steadily moved him toward the river, and that was probably good because he would have a hard time running out of the field. On the other hand, heavy groves of trees lined the river and he certainly didn't want to land in a tangle of branches where there was no way he could escape from such a dangerous mess. He started pulling on the left side of his chute, attempting to land at the edge of the trees.

Jack could see cars and trucks off in the distance moving steadily toward the river and into the open field. The Nazis had to have spotted him coming down, and were sending in their troops! Not only did he have to land without breaking a leg or getting dragged into the river, now he had half of the enemy's army bearing down on him!

Jack watched apprehensively as the vehicles turned in his direction. Obviously he was a sitting duck that could be spotted from any angle. A good marksman could line him up in the crosshairs of a rifle's scope, and Captain Martin would be dead before his feet even touched the ground!

Picking an open area at the edge of the trees, Jack jerked right and left on the straps to guide the parachute to that exact spot. About ten feet from the ground, a gust of wind swept through the trees, grabbing the parachute and jerking it hard to the left. Jack lost all control and could only hang on. When he hit the field, the pain in his legs became electric, plunging him straight into the ground. The wind hurled the parachute forward, and dragged Jack's face through the soil, forcing dirt up his nose and into his mouth. He spit and sputtered.

Choking and coughing, Martin realized he could either be dragged farther out into the field or possibly back into the river if he didn't get out of the chute's harness. The only jumps he'd made in the past had all been practice and nothing of this nature had ever happened, but now he was faced with a real dilemma. Not stopping the effects of the wind could turn the landing into as big a disaster as the Messerschmitts' attacks earlier that morning.

With a wrenching pull, Jack attempted to unsnap the harness. The chute slightly collapsed and slowed down. Rolling sideways, he managed to get one strap of the parachute off. After several gut-wrenching twists, he lowered the billowing chute to the ground and managed to get himself free. The wind picked up again, blowing the chute out toward the field and away from him.

Jack lay in the dirt panting and feeling the endless throbbing in his legs, but he knew he couldn't stay there long. The Nazis would be all over that field in a matter of minutes, and his only hope was to get into the grove of trees near the river.

With all his might, he pushed himself up from the ground, and started to run. After only a couple of steps, Jack fell again. The damage to his legs apparently was even greater than he thought. He hurt so badly that he wanted to die out there in that lonely field, but he knew that wasn't on his list of options. Pushing with his elbows, he started crawling toward the trees.

Off in the distance, dogs barked fiercely and he could hear German soldiers yelling as well as the roar of their trucks. They weren't close yet, but they soon would be. Rolling over on his back, he stared up at the blue sky with clouds leisurely drifting by. He had no way to escape. A trickle of sweat started running down the side of his face. Jack Martin was finished.

———

Arnwolf Mandel's roadster roared over the backcountry, flying down the dirt roads dividing one farm from the next. The flat countryside offered few distractions other than deep bumps and erosions caused by a recent rain. Driven by his aide Karl Herrick, the SS officer's Mercedes bumped off the road and sped through a large cornfield to catch up with Colonel Bern Schmidt's troops already chasing the parachutes drifting down out of the sky. The roadster clipped through the field like a sickle, sending cornstalks flying in every direction. Mandel felt certain at least three of the Allied airman had been captured and shot by now. He wanted to be there for the kill when the last couple of men were rounded up.

"I see the swine!" Mandel pointed straight ahead. "See those parachutes above the trees. They're coming down fast."

"I'm driving as rapidly as I can," Herrick groused. "We don't want to get killed by running into some hidden ditch that could wreck the car."

"Put away all reluctance!" Arnwolf shot back. "This is an opportunity to demonstrate your commitment to *Der Führer*."

Herrick said nothing, but clenched the wheel tightly and

pushed the gas pedal to the floor. The car surged forward, tearing long green cornstalks out of the ground and shattering them in a thousand pieces.

Mandel smiled as he always did when pushing someone to the edge. Herrick knew better than to talk back and would do as he was ordered. At the same time, Mandel recognized Herrick had a point. If they got mired into a heap of dirt, they'd miss the entire party. He leaned forward to watch more carefully where they were going. At the end of the field, the car came flying out into another section of farm land.

After ripping completely across some farmer's cornfield, the Mercedes barely inched through a stone gateway that Schmidt's men had left open. Herrick threw the car into second and started through the barren field.

"Start honking!" Arnwolf demanded. "Slow them down so we can catch up."

Karl Herrick lay on the horn. Some of the *Wehrmacht* troops turned and watched them approach. Mandel adjusted his hat to look as proficient as possible. Herrick turned slightly to the left to pull up alongside a touring car that must be carrying the officers in charge. Mandel had the car door open before his roadster had even pulled to a complete stop.

"*Mein* Colonel!" Mandel saluted smartly. "I left my office at once."

Colonel Bern Schmidt returned the salute. "You made amazing time, Officer Mandel. You got here soon enough for the kill." He pointed at one final parachute settling to the ground. "That's the last of the sorry lot. Unfortunately, this cornfield was recently plowed and we can drive no further, but walking only heightens the chase."

Arnwolf covered his eyes, watching the last parachute disappear into the clump of trees. He withdrew his 9mm Pistolen-08, commonly called a Luger, and dramatically shanked the pistol to make sure it was ready to fire.

"Our ground troops will rush from the far end while we attack straight ahead," Colonel Schmidt said, pointing toward the trees. "Shouldn't be much of a problem to capture them."

"Or *kill them!*" Mandel added.

Schmidt eyed the SS officer with caution, as if he didn't want any mistakes that could backfire and get some of his own men killed.

"I'm ready," Mandel urged, and pointed to a tall, thin young man standing next to one of the colonel's soldiers. "We've got a guide for this foray?"

Colonel Schmidt smiled cynically. "Young Dirk Vogel wasn't exactly eager to help us. He's the son of the farmer who owns this land."

Mandel glanced at the young man standing there in a long white shirt and the typical work pants of the farm. The boy looked about nineteen or twenty years old and didn't impress the SS officer. Arnwolf shrugged.

"But Vogel's going to help us," Colonel Schmidt said, and glared at the farm boy. "Aren't you, son?"

Dirk Vogel nodded obediently, but didn't look enthusiastic.

"Okay, let's go get them." Colonel Schmidt pointed to the north and swung his hand to send the men onward. Twenty-five German soldiers heaved their rifles off their shoulders, and started a cautious march toward the trees.

"Remember they are armed," Schmidt warned. "We must assume they will shoot."

"Not if *I* see them first," Arnwolf Mandel growled.

CHAPTER THREE

*B*ecause the recently plowed Belgium farm field left the soil turned in clumps, large clods of soil pressed into Captain Martin's back. Dirt remained so loose that dust kept blowing in every direction. Off in the distance, Martin could still hear dogs barking, and knew the Germans would be there quickly. Although his legs felt like they had been barbecued and wouldn't work right, he had to get out of the field. Rolling over on his stomach, Jack started using his elbows to pull himself through the dirt. Laboriously and slowly, he started dragging his body toward the trees that lined the river. After crawling a couple of feet, he wondered if anything he did would make any real difference. Even if he got into the trees, what would keep the Nazis from grabbing him?

Jack pushed forward a couple more feet and realized he couldn't go any farther. His strength was gone; his energy spent and the pain too great. Then again, if he was going to die out in that field, it wouldn't be without a fight. He pushed forward and fell on his face.

Abruptly a pair of strong hands grabbed the back of his coat and dragged him forward. The Germans had him! Jack struggled to roll to one side to see who was pulling him.

"Hello, kid!"

Martin's mouth dropped. Hank Holt had pulled him out of the dirt!

"Looks like you could use a hand from your old navigator. I didn't think lying out in the dirt served the dignity of your office."

"Hank!" Jack grabbed his flight jacket. "Where'd you come from?"

"I jumped behind you and was the last man to land. You probably didn't look up and notice I was nearly coming down on top of you. I landed in the trees."

"The Germans are out there!" Jack pointed behind him. "They're coming fast!"

"Yeah, I noticed that little problem. Listen to me carefully, Jack. I'm going to have to drag you into the river. We'll hide under the bank somewhere. It may hurt, but it's our only chance."

Captain Martin nodded his head resolutely. "I understand. Sorry, Hank. I simply can't stand up."

"No problem. I'll drag you into the water."

Hank Holt grabbed Jack Martin under both armpits and pulled him backward through the trees. After about ten feet, Hank found a narrow opening down into the water. Without stopping, he jerked Martin to the edge of the bank, and then down into the cold water. Holding his friend with his arm across Martin's chest, Holt let the strong current carry them downstream. After only fifteen feet he spotted an indentation where the undertow had cut a hole in the bank, and pushed Martin inside.

The water level allowed both men to keep their heads barely above the water and still breathe.

"I can't believe it," Jack whispered. "My legs instantly feel a hundred percent better. The water is taking all the burning out."

"Good! Good. Shut up. Don't talk."

"I know," Jack said. "But it's still amazing!"

Both men held on and listened. Barking dogs suddenly sounded like they were just above them. Jack could hear the soldiers yelling, and was certain they were onto them. Over his head, he heard the steps as men ran by. He gritted his teeth. Surely they had been found!

———

German Shepherd dogs strained at their leashes, trying to charge into the trees. The barking and snapping sounded like the animals were poised to tear the enemy into a thousand pieces. The dog handlers stayed in crouched positions in case the Americans were hiding behind some tree ready to shoot them. Other German soldiers rushed into position so their attack would be unified.

Colonel Bern Schmidt walked carefully and slowly toward the trees with SS Officer Mandel following behind him. Wearing one of the traditional steel helmets that came down over his ears, Schmidt had quickly recognized that Arnwolf Mandel talked a better story than he performed. Once the assault began, Mandel allowed others to become shields for him. Nevertheless, Schmidt maintained his pace toward the river, pushing the assault unit forward.

The Sambre Meuse River had always been important to both France and Belgium. Its connection to the Albert Canal provided a direct route to Antwerp and Zeeland, opening finally to the North Sea. The wide river was always lined with towering trees and thick bushes that provided a good place for anyone to hide. Schmidt anticipated that the Americans would probably run in the direction of Liège, hoping to get to the Ardennes Forest where they would disappear into the thick underbrush. The Allies probably had no idea that Germany's Army Group A had already sent their 4 Army units into the area. If Schmidt's men didn't get the Allies, 4 Army certainly would.

"Into the trees!" Colonel Schmidt ordered. "Pay attention!"

Troops with rifles rushed ahead of Schmidt and Mandel, breaking into the trees. With precision, the *Wehrmacht* units moved into formation and then broke into a search posture along the river banks.

"Here's one parachute!" a soldier yelled from the field.

Colonel Schmidt looked over his shoulder. Sixty feet away the trooper stood holding a white parachute up in the air. Schmidt signaled he saw it and then motioned the man to join them in the trees. As he approached the tree line, Schmidt pulled Dirk Vogel alongside of him. For a moment he studied the long-armed young man. With a head full of tousled blonde hair, Vogel looked like any other Dutch boy working a farm, but Schmidt wasn't fooled. Vogel wasn't on their side of this war and couldn't be trusted.

"You paying attention?" Schmidt demanded.

"Yes, sir," Vogel answered timidly.

"Then get into those trees and find those cowering soldiers!"

Vogel reluctantly pushed through the underbrush and started walking down the shoreline. Dragging his feet, like a lazy schoolboy, he still walked along at a brisk pace. Pointing in the direction of Liège, Vogel kept moving.

Liège? Schmidt thought to himself. *At least Vogel is going in the right direction. Give him more time. We'll see.*

Without looking back, Vogel kept walking south in increasingly long steps. Arnwolf Mandel matched his strides but stayed to the back of the unit. Bern Schmidt kept observing the scene with quick glances to the right and left. After walking a mile downstream, Schmidt shouted for Vogel to stop.

"Where are you going?" the colonel demanded.

"I don't think they could swim across the river without us seeing them," Dirk Vogel explained. "They would have to stay on this side of the river. My guess is that they'd aim toward the Ardennes."

Colonel Schmidt watched the young man's eyes. Nothing seemed amiss or out of place, and Vogel was making sense. Maybe the boy wasn't misleading them, but Schmidt wasn't certain. He didn't want some Dutch child to confuse his unit. The Dutch were Aryans, but they still hadn't gotten the idea of what this war was about.

"You want me to keep going?" Vogel asked apprehensively.

"Yes," Schmidt said slowly. "Keep moving."

Once more Vogel started down the river.

Cool river water splashed into the American's face, erasing all sense of time. Jack Martin had no idea the length of time they had been in the river. Regardless of how many hours had passed, the water had been a soothing relief on his burned legs that had been more than welcome. A warm summer left the Sambre Meuse River on the pleasant side, so the long wait in hiding had proved durable. Unfortunately, the river water had ruined his wristwatch, so there was no way to tell the hour. The same thing had happened to Hank Holt.

Periodically Holt ducked out of their hiding spot to check if the Germans were still hunting them. While he hadn't heard any noise for a considerable period of time, the silence didn't mean the Jerries couldn't be hiding around the shoreline with their guns cocked. Hank noted where the sun seemed to be sinking. By now he was estimating it must be midafternoon at the least.

The two men said nothing, but waited, periodically pumping their legs to stay back against the bank. To kill time, Jack tried to think about something, anything. He had to keep stagnation from sending his bright mind flying off into a panic. The whole experience had been far, far too unsettling. Eventually he started reflecting on his childhood years in Amarillo, Texas.

The dust bowl days of the '30s had proved a disastrous time for most of the farmers. Drought conditions had dried out the Texas flat country until nothing but yellow stubble remained. Howling winds blew up off the flat, arid plains, sending dust and dirt into the sky so profusely that the sun virtually disappeared behind opaque clouds of red and brown soil hurtling down the prairie. Everyone struggled to endure and many didn't, but the Martin family somehow managed to hang on. Probably old Granddad Hennie Matthys had hammered into Walter, Jack's father, that endurance remained paramount.

Bobbing up and down in the river, Jack forced himself to remember *"endurance remains paramount."*

In the late '30s Martin's family had joined the "America First" rallies, a movement opposing war with Europe. Though they didn't mention it often, the entire clan remained uncomfortable with the idea of going to war against Germany because of their family ties. Moreover, European countries had been in a thousand wars over and over again across the centuries. Americans needed to take care of themselves and leave the Europeans to do the same. At least that had always been Walter Martin's thinking.

But the attack on Pearl Harbor changed everything. In a matter of hours the world became totally different. No longer could they ignore the staggering threat dumped at their own front door. Jack Martin left the farm without one shred of reluctance and joined the Army without a second thought. He had read those pronouncements from Hitler that the objective of the Axis forces was the annihilation of the English, French, and Belgium armies. Hitler could talk endlessly of fighting with a "spirit of holy hatred," but what he would discover was that the Texas farm boys didn't need any loud-mouthed propaganda to prove that they were tougher than the Nazi bullies.

"Look!" Hank Holt abruptly whispered and jerked on Martin's arm. "A flat-bottomed boat is coming downstream!"

Jack froze in place. The water was clear enough that anyone who came within a few feet of them might recognize their forms hiding in the river. He pushed against the mud of the river bank to hang on without making any movement.

"Sh-h-h," Hank cautioned. "The boat's getting closer."

Jack swallowed hard. He hadn't thought they'd get this far anyway. How terrible to be picked off just when they had a real chance to escape. Taking a deep breath, he squinted his eyes and hung on.

The flat-bottomed boat slowly edged along the bank, and then stopped parallel to the two Americans. Hank Holt raised his hands, and walked out of the hiding place. Jack followed him with his hands also raised.

To Jack's surprise, a tall, long-armed adolescent stared back at them. "Get into the boat," the young man said with a distinctive British accent. "We do not have much time."

"Who . . . who are you?" Jack asked in amazement.

"Dirk," the young man said. "My name is Dirk Vogel."

CHAPTER FOUR

The young Dutchman pulled the American soldiers into his flat-bottomed boat and threw a dirty tarp over them. With skillful probing of his long steering pole, he started navigating the boat into the river. "Keep down and only whisper. If they see or hear us, we're all dead."

"How'd you find us?" Captain Martin whispered from under the tarp.

"I saw the scratches on the ground where someone had been pulled into the river," Dirk Vogel said. "The Germans never paid any attention to the marks trailing down to the water. They kept expecting you to pop up behind a bush or a tree. I dragged my feet over the area when I walked past to mess up the scrapes in the dirt. You were more than lucky that the Germans kept looking straight ahead and didn't look down."

"That's putting it mildly," Hank Holt said from the other side of the tarp. "When your boat pulled up, we thought you were the Jerries."

"They've gone way downstream," Dirk said. "But you can't take anything for granted. They might double back and show up around one of these bends. The Nazis can be crafty."

"They gave up because the Germans thought we escaped?" Martin asked.

"Far from it," Dirk said. "They caught three other men who bailed out of your bomber first and shot them. The Nazis have no heart."

"Killed them!" Martin nearly came out from under the tarp.

"Stay down *and whisper*," Dirk warned. "You can't take any chances." He kept maneuvering the boat through the swift current with strong, certain pushes of his stout steering pole.

"But . . . but . . . ," Jack mumbled.

"Yes, sometimes they take Allied prisoners, and sometimes they kill them. Depends on the disposition of the people in charge. This time the *Wehrmacht* was angry and the Gestapo was searching for them. A bad combination of two evils."

For a long time Jack said nothing, but his temper boiled. Killing men landing in parachutes was nothing other than murder. Every value he held was challenged by these Nazi beasts.

"Why'd you come back after us?" Hank Holt finally asked. "You put yourself in danger."

"I'm part of the underground. It's our job to help people like you escape. My family lends their farm to this effort."

"Rather on the dangerous side," Hank observed.

"Not if we're not caught," Vogel chuckled.

"But how come you were with the Nazis *first?*" Martin asked with a hint of suspicion in his voice.

"They know our family farm is adjacent to the river, and I know this river like the back of my hand. That's why I caught your marks in the dirt. Early this morning the Nazis came by and picked up me and my father when the report came in that they were attacking your airplanes. Father went with the group that scoured the other side of the river. He was there when they caught your men and killed them."

"Did your father return safely?" Hank asked.

"They let him go once the Nazis finished their dirty work. My group went much farther downstream because they couldn't find you. The SS officer finally became angry, but eventually Colonel Schmidt's men brought me back to our farm. Believe me when I tell you that these officers will not stop looking for you."

After several minutes of thinking about what Dirk had said, Jack asked, "And exactly what does it mean that this patrol will keep chasing us?"

"You are marked!" Dirk said. "Unless you get out of this country, you are walking dead men."

The two men settled into silence, thinking about what they had heard. Neither wanted to ask any more questions for the time being. Dirk kept working the boat back toward the Vogel farm. A hush fell over the wide river.

Constantly looking up and down both sides of the river, Dirk Vogel said nothing. He poled his flat-bottomed boat toward the edge of the family farm. Having only been in the underground for six months, he hadn't done much more than convey messages and run errands. Pulling the two Americans out of the river had been his first attempt at actually saving anyone shot down over Belgium. Dirk had the usual Dutch emotional disposition that didn't show much sentiment, but his feelings had churned like a plunger making butter when he hauled the two men into his boat. Anyone watching through the trees could have seen them. Such escape work remained extremely dangerous.

Dirk kept pushing the boat. He wasn't far from the shoreline where a narrow path wound up to the Vogel barn. Three generations back, the Vogels came down from the North country up around Groningen and settled south of Maastrich where a good number of French people farmed. Belgium had been shaped by the Protestant Reformation wars that left Protestants in Holland and pushed the Roman Catholics into Belgium. The people living around the Vogel farm had always been a mixture of Dutch and French, who started listening to the British Broadcasting Company when radio became popular. Consequently, they all spoke English with a British accent. Common people like these farmers worked hard to scrape out a living.

"We'll be at the farm shortly," Dirk said softly. "Stay down and keep quiet."

The two Americans said nothing.

Dirk knew his parents would be quick to offer medical attention to the injured soldier. Groot and Lina weren't happy about his work with the underground, but they understood how important it was to resist the Nazis and reluctantly agreed to Dirk's involvement.

"Remember," Dirk said over his shoulder, "you must not move a muscle until I give you the okay sign. I'd call, but I don't want to put my family in any danger."

No one answered.

Vogel poled up to the bank of the river, and tied his boat to a small dock he and his father had built. Stretching out by the dock, he waited to see what would happen. If the Germans were watching him or circulating in the area, a few quiet moments would give him time to act natural and make sure no one sneaked up on them.

Dirk stared at his reflection in the Sambre Meuse River. His entire life had been spent as a quiet farm boy doing what every other farm boy did. He got up early, helped with chores, went to school, came home, and returned to more work. Dirk loved his parents, Groot and Lina, and tried to be a faithful, obedient son. Their home was quiet and peaceful most of the time. At least that had been true until the invasions began in May 1940. For the last three years their world had been turned upside down and inside out. Explosive chaos had brought an end to the predictable order of things and changed Dirk's mind about the value of trying to maintain the tranquility of the countryside.

The shift in his thinking started one Sunday in their local Reformed Church. Most of the area churches were Roman

Catholic, but because of the heavy Dutch population around the Vogel farm a pastor had come down from Tilburg in the Netherlands, and a new congregation began a couple of decades earlier. Just before the German invasions, a pastor named Harold Assink showed up to shepherd the local flock. A tall, thin man with dark hair, Rev. Assink turned out to be a passionate, fiery preacher. The Vogels always sat in church paying rapt attention to everything he said.

Back in March when it was so cold, with lots of snow on the ground, Rev. Assink had started a series on the Sermon on the Mount. Standing behind the large, carved pulpit, Assink loudly proclaimed, "Blessed are you when others revile you and persecute you and utter all kinds of evil against you falsely on my account. Rejoice and be glad, for your reward is great in heaven, for so they persecuted the prophets who were before you." Rev. Assink walked around to the side of the mahogany pulpit and stared pointedly at the congregation. Dirk believed the pastor was looking straight into his heart. He took a deep breath and hung on to the pew.

"Make no mistake about it!" Harold Assink rammed his closed fist straight up toward the church ceiling. "Christians can't avoid a collision with evil! None of us can avoid or shirk from our responsibility." The preacher swung his fist toward the congregation. "Evil comes in many shapes and sizes. Sometimes it's temptation, family problems, personal relationships," he took a deep breath, and said in a low voice, "and other times it's political." Assink stopped for a moment and let the words sink in.

"We can't make our choices based on what we'd like to choose. Circumstances frame the problem for us. We have to make our decisions based on what is *in front of our eyes*, remembering that our ultimate hope must be set on what is in heaven!"

It wasn't what the pastor said, but what he implied that had grabbed Dirk's attention. No one could say that Rev. Assink was dabbling in politics, but everyone knew his persuasion. The minister hated the Nazis! Dirk concluded the pastor was suggesting that maybe the Scripture supported being involved with the underground to resist the invaders. Joining up was the right thing to do.

At that moment Dirk came to the conclusion he'd been thinking about for weeks. He was going to join the French-Belgian resistance organization that helped Allied soldiers escape from behind the lines. Such a heady decision could cost him his life. Still, Dirk believed that Christ had called him to stand for what was right even if the conflict plunged him into persecution.

After the services when the family filed out of the church, Dirk shook the minister's hand and looked deep into his eyes. "You've helped me with an important decision this morning," Dirk's voice cracked slightly. "Thank you."

Harold Assink studied Dirk's face critically and carefully for several moments. "Good!" he answered. "You be careful now, young Vogel."

Dirk had walked out of that Sunday morning service into a new life. The quiet, steady world of farming had become electric with unpredictable and most unsteady experiences exploding everyday. Not once had he ever looked back.

The massive river whirled past. Enough time had passed waiting for the Germans to make a move. Since they hadn't, Dirk felt certain he could move the men up to the hiding place in the barn. With his foot he pulled the tarp back.

"Let's go!" Dirk said, and started walking. "Time to move."

Hank Holt put his shoulder under Jack Martin's arm and helped him up the narrow trail.

"Faster," Dirk demanded. "You mustn't be seen."

The Gestapo's outer office in Maastrich remained a highly efficient model of order and decorum. Arnwolf Mandel demanded the secretaries perform at a constant level of high proficiency, keeping the clutter of superfluous papers and letters carefully tucked away in their desks. If an SS official from Berlin walked in unexpectedly, the senior officer would find the room fit for *Der Führer's* own feet!

The inner office was another matter.

Stacks of files sat around Arnwolf's private office leaving the appearance of a world in shambles. Limp coats lay piled over chairs for days while unnecessary stacks of books, clutter, and junk remained all over the floor. A black fedora hung randomly from the corner of a bookcase. Four empty coffee cups stood on end tables, sitting in odd positions. The private world of Arnwolf Mandel remained quite to the contrary of his public mania for order.

Arnwolf Mandel paced nervously back and forth across his private office. Obviously irritated and angry, Arnwolf remained furious that Schmidt's squad of troops hadn't captured the last two fleeing Allied soldiers. Impulsively he kicked an umbrella lying on the floor, sending it flying across the disheveled room. Mandel's great plans for what to do with the trophies of war had now gone sour and that made Arnwolf decidedly unhappy.

If the Berlin office learned that Mandel had been on the scene when two fleeing prisoners escaped, it certainly wouldn't be good for his reputation. While Colonel Bern Schmidt considered the chase simply another day's work, Arnwolf took the matter as a personal affront. He was not about to let these scavengers that dropped out of the sky flop out of the fishnet Mandel had thrown across the locale. While the Maastrich office had to maintain the normal demands of their secret surveillance of the public, he had concluded that chasing and catching these two Allied soldiers was the most important task life had ever given him. Mandel now had a new burning cause that he intended to pursue with a fury.

"Ah, sir," his aide Karl Herrick said, opening the outer door slightly. "I don't mean to interrupt you."

Arnwolf glared at him. Slightly balding, Herrick wore circular glasses on his long nose, giving him a bookwormish appearance. Quite to the contrary, Herrick had the potential to be vicious. Most of the time he walked around the office with that beaten hangdog look on his face that Mandel hated.

"What is it?" Arnwolf snapped.

"I have these documents that just came in from Berlin." Karl held up a handful of papers. "They are surveillance forms to be filled out when our observation of suspects is completed."

"Come in and shut the door." Mandel motioned for Herrick to take a seat in front of him.

Karl walked quickly to his place.

Mandel cursed. "Yes, yes. Take care of those forms! What I actually want you to do is focus on the *real business* of this office."

"Yes, sir."

"We must not give up on catching those Allied flyboys that escaped us today." Mandel pounded his desk. "I want the capture of those men to be your *primary* task. We must do *whatever is necessary* to run those dogs down."

"Yes, sir," Herrick repeated himself and pulled out his notebook to write any instructions down.

"Bern Schmidt can go home and jump in bed if he wishes! But we're not going to sleep until we've apprehended those two criminals! They have to be out there somewhere where we can still put our hands on them. Understand me?"

Herrick only nodded his head.

"I didn't trust that Dutch farm boy either and I still don't!" Mandel started pacing and rubbing his fat chin. "I think we need to organize our own Gestapo-style chase to round up these characters. Leave the *Wehrmacht* out of it!"

Herrick rubbed his neck nervously. "Do we want to make that statement in public—"

"Of course not!" Mandel cut him off. "We are having a confidential conversation!" He glared at the assistant. "I want you to start lining up men we can trust for another run across the countryside."

"Yes, sir."

"We're going to scour that river bottom once again. I want every tree, bush, and building looked in, under, and around until we turn up those two soldiers! Am I clear?"

"Most definitely!"

"Good! We must develop our own investigative techniques until we've honed our search approach down to a fine edge. We may miss these two men, but we'll be ready next time. I want this office to set a record that the entire Gestapo will recognize. We must lead every organization in the Third Reich in capturing escapees!"

Karl Herrick kept nodding and scribbling on his small pad. "Yes . . . yes," he repeated.

"Okay! Get out there and accomplish what I told you to do!"

Herrick nodded perfunctorily. "Yes, sir," he repeated for the last time and darted out the door, shutting it immediately behind him.

"I want them to remember me," Arnwolf said to himself, "to remember that I was determined and persistent to the end. I will climb the ladder to the top of the Reich by annihilating every enemy regardless of who I have to kill." He snarled malevolently. "Let the world learn to pay attention to the name of Arnwolf Mandel!"

CHAPTER FIVE

While Hank Holt and Jack Martin slept hidden under a haystack in the barn, the roar of bombers flying overhead along with distant explosions shook the Vogels' house during the night. Plaster dropped from the ceiling in the kitchen and the windows rattled. The ground-shaking repercussions remained far enough away that Groot Vogel believed the Allies must be bombing the Eben-Emael Fort or possibly installations along the Albert Canal. Eventually Dirk crept down the stairs and tried to sleep in the cellar, but Groot and Lina knew that if a bomb hit their house, the basement would be gone in a flash. Lina stood at their upstairs window, watching the orange and red explosions on the horizon.

"I don't think we can leave those soldiers out there under a stack of hay," Lina finally said. "It's too dangerous."

"Yeah," Groot groaned. "Come back to bed."

"I suppose we have no alternative tonight." Lina crawled back into their large feather bed. "But we must tend to the problem in the morning."

Being staunch Calvinists, the Vogels rolled over and eventually went back to sleep, believing the matter remained in God's hands.

Mornings always came early for farmers. Attending the animals took precedence before breakfast. After completing the chores, Dirk finally walked into the kitchen and left his wooden shoes by the door. The table was already set.

"The cows are okay?" Groot asked.

"Yes," Dirk said, sitting down before a bowl of steaming oatmeal. "No problems."

"And your friends?" Lina glanced apprehensively over her shoulder toward the door. "No problems under the haystack?"

"A little stuffy. That's all."

Groot and Lina exchanged a knowing glance, and everybody started eating silently. After a couple of minutes Groot picked up a freshly sliced thick piece of bread and watched his son out of the corner of his eye.

"That boy's legs doing any better?" Groot asked.

"No," Dirk answered, "He's got a big problem. The man struggles even to walk."

"Hmm," Groot chewed on the bread. "I think we need to move those boys. The bombing makes the barn too dangerous a facility to hide someone."

Dirk glanced at both parents to ascertain if everyone seemed to be in agreement. Lina showed no sign of resistance to the idea.

"I think we need to move those boys inside our house," Groot continued. "That feller with the burns needs to be out of the elements."

"But Papa," Dirk protested. "Our house is too small. If the Gestapo made a raid, they'd find those men instantly."

"Well," Groot smiled, "every family has its little secrets." He winked at Lina. "We thought that you would have discovered the hidden area in our basement long before now, but even you haven't found the hidden space."

"Basement?" Dirk frowned. "What are you talking about?"

Lina scooped another heaping tablespoon of oatmeal into Dirk's bowl. "There's a space behind the basement wall where two men could hide quite easily. Didn't know that, did you?"

"A space?" Dirk scratched his head. "Where?"

"Son," Groot said, "when you scoot that shelf of canned goods back from the wall, there's a small piece of wood behind it. A man can crawl behind the wall through that covered opening."

"I've never noticed it!" Dirk stood up. "Of course I never moved the shelf out from the wall either. I'll look and see."

"Later," Groot said and motioned for him to stay sitting down. "I believe before this day gets started you need to go out and move those soldiers downstairs. No telling when the Gestapo or the German Army could come back through here. We need to bring the men inside early this morning."

Dirk pushed back from the table. "Yes. You are absolutely right. I will go out and fetch them right now."

"And I will move the shelf of canned vegetables away from the wall while you do," Groot said. "We need to be swift about it."

Dirk quickly gobbled down the oatmeal his mother had dished up for him, wiped his mouth, slipped on his wooden shoes, and hurried out the back door. Far above him he could hear the roar of airplane engines. Dirk stopped and stared.

A German-Focke Wulf 190 appeared to be zooming in and out, attacking an RAF Blenheim bomber probably returning from an early morning strike deep in the heart of Germany. The German fighter plane kept making angling attacks on the larger bomber. Obviously both airplanes were locked in a fight to the death.

Dirk shaded his eyes to study carefully what happened.

The Focke Wulf made a sharp angular turn and descended on top of the bomber. A piece of the long wing broke loose and smoke started bellowing from the engines. Instantly the bomber turned into a dive toward the ground. In seconds the side door flew open and four men dived out. Parachutes opened and the Allied survivors drifted toward the ground. Once again they were coming down close enough to the Vogel's farm that Dirk would have to pay attention.

"Got to get Captain Martin and Lieutenant Holt down to the basement," Dirk said to himself and started running toward the barn. "We're going to have a busy day at the Vogel farm."

SS Officer Karl Herrick pulled Arnwolf Mandel's car into the bushes near the river. From this vantage point Mandel could study the house with his binoculars. A truckload of twenty armed men dressed in civilian clothes pulled up behind them. Mandel signaled for everyone to be quiet.

"This morning's report indicated an RAF Blenheim bomber was shot down not far from here and the *Wehrmacht's* been chasing the survivors for the last six hours," Mandel told Herrick. "Haven't caught them." Mandel spit on the ground. "The only logical place for anyone in this area to be hiding is that farmhouse." He pointed up the hill.

"Yes, sir," Herrick answered as quietly as possible.

Mandel studied the house with his binoculars. "I can't see much from here," he said. "Looks like a man and a woman walking around in there."

"That's where that Vogel boy lives," Herrick added.

"And there's a barn over there. You take half the men and circle the outbuilding. Turn it upside down."

"Absolutely," Herrick answered.

"I'll take the other half and assault the house. Let's move!"

Karl Herrick always became more animated when left on his own. His compliant, passive countenance turned into an aggressive attack mode during a relentless pursuit. Holding his Luger tightly, Herrick motioned for half the men to follow him.

Herrick's unit of ten made a sweep through the underbrush before rushing the old barn. Herrick led the charge, dashing into the shed without stopping. The barn wasn't large and probably kept only five milk cows at the most. Hay was stacked around the building with one large pile next to the back wall. Without a moment's hesitation, the eleven men scoured the barn. Only one area remained untouched. The large stack of hay.

Herrick snapped his fingers and motioned for one of the men with a bayonet attached to his rifle to rush the haystack. The young man looked apprehensive and reluctant. Karl Herrick gave him a "now or never" stare. After a long deep breath, he charged the haystack with his bayonet, aiming at a low level.

"A-a-a-h!" a scream erupted from inside the haystack. A man staggered forward, sending hay flying in every direction.

The SS agent with the bayonet jumped back in shock.

Herrick aimed his pistol at the soldier, staring at the figure sprawled on the ground in front of him. The bayonet had caught the British soldier in the thigh, leaving a dark red stain spreading across his pant leg. The soldier kept rolling on the ground in pain.

"Who are you?" Herrick asked in his limited English.

"I'm ... I'm ... from England," the soldier struggled to speak. "With the Royal Air Force."

"Get him!" Herrick ordered his crew. "Drag this swine back around to the front of the house."

"Ple-a-s-e," the British soldier pleaded. "I'm hurt."

"Not like you are going to be!" Herrick said.

Arnwolf's men surrounded the farmhouse but saw nothing unusual. Mandel hung back, allowing his men to stay in front of him. With a dramatic lunge, one of the larger men hit the front door, smashing it into pieces on the floor in front of him. A woman in the kitchen screamed and ran for another room.

"Grab her!" Arnwolf ordered. "Search the house quickly!"

SS agents rushed into the farmhouse while Mandel stood outside at a safe distance from the chaos, but watching intensely. After a couple of minutes his men brought Lina out and moments later dragged Groot through the smashed door. Groot stood outside with his black cap in his hand.

"We didn't find anyone else," one of the men said.

"You checked every room ... the basement?" Arnwolf demanded.

"Every place!"

"There was no boy in the house?" Mandel puzzled. "Hmm."

"These two are all we found."

Mandel rubbed his fat chin. He didn't like the looks of the situation. The SS officer would have laid money on the possibility of finding Allied soldiers hiding in the house. "I don't understand," he muttered to himself, and waved over his shoulder to signal for his vehicles to drive up the road to where they were standing.

Lina Vogel stood bent over with her arms across her chest, looking terrified. Her husband appeared more angry than afraid. The couple huddled together defensively.

Mandel felt uncomfortable and angry like he had when Colonel Schmidt gave up the chase the day before. A second failure in two days made everything worse.

"Hey!" Karl Herrick called from the barn. "We caught one!"

Arnwolf Mandel whirled around. To his amazement two of Herrick's men were dragging a man between them. Blood ran down the Allied prisoner's pant leg and the man looked as intimidated as the Vogels did.

"Caught him hiding in the haystack," Herrick said, running up to his boss. "But this Brit was the only one we found."

"British?" Mandel mused. "Then he can't be an escapee from yesterday."

"Afraid not," Herrick said, "but we did get one of the bail-outs from the Blenheim bomber. That's more than the army accomplished."

"Yes," Arnwolf said thoughtfully. "Maybe we can make his escape fit into my plans, anyway." He beckoned for his men to bring Groot closer to him. The truck and Mandel's car pulled up on the edge of the open area in front of the Vogel farmhouse.

An SS agent grabbed Groot by the shirt and jerked him forward into the center of the area in front of the farmhouse.

"You know this escapee?" Mandel asked the Dutchman, pointing toward the pilot.

Groot only shook his head.

"I can't hear you!" Mandel sounded.

"No," Groot mumbled.

Mandel studied Groot's eyes. Arnwolf didn't detect any lying. Vogel probably hadn't seen the British pilot before. Maybe the Brit simply found his way into the barn while fleeing his captors. Such a scenario fit the situation. Mandel guessed the Dutchman was telling the truth.

"I don't believe you," Mandel answered coldly. "We will not tolerate collaborators. No longer will you be allowed to violate our laws or hospitality."

Arnwolf Mandel raised his pistol and shot Groot Vogel square in the middle of his forehead. Without making a sound Vogel toppled backward; his black hat bounced on the ground.

"No!" Lina screamed. "No! Not my husband!"

Without saying another word, Arnwolf turned to the British soldier and shot him square in the middle of the chest. The man gasped and slumped to his knees before falling face forward on the ground.

"Put their bodies in the back of the truck," Mandel ordered Herrick. "Stack 'em in and let's get out of here. We'll dispose of them in town."

The SS agents quickly slung the two dead men into the back of their truck. Nobody said anything. Only the sobs of Lina Vogel rang through the air. The men immediately filled the vehicles and the engines roared to life.

"We'll take the bodies back to the town square and make a spectacle out of Vogel," Mandel said. "His body hanging upside down from a tree ought to scare any traitors helping these swine escape."

The car pulled in front of the truck and Mandel looked over his shoulder. Lina Vogel lay in a heap on the ground, sobbing and hold her husband's black hat. She clutched the cap against her breast as if it were her most treasured possession in the world.

"Hope we didn't make a mistake," Herrick said.

Mandel said nothing, but stared straight ahead.

PART TWO

Escape in the Dark

CHAPTER SIX

Madame Ann Brusselman had no distinguishing features that would keep her from appearing anything but average. A rather plain woman and with her dark brown hair pulled back tightly on her head, she looked like only one of the crowd hustling back and forth in the marketplace. Of French descent, she and Julien had lived in Brussels, Belgium, all of their married lives. On the overweight side, Julien had the same nameless look that would make it difficult to identify and remember his face when anyone passed him in the street. Their outstanding quality was anonymity.

Along with their two children, Ann and Julien lived on the second floor of 127 Rue d'Ixelles. Twelve-year-old Yvonne had eyes like her father, and Jacques's eight-year-old face bore the characteristics of his mother. With the easy, confident manner of most children of their age, Jacques and Yvonne's lives were far more complex than they seemed. The two slightly built children were part of their parents' elaborate endeavors to assist Allied soldiers in escaping the Germans.

At three o'clock in the afternoon, Ann hustled around their apartment, dusting the furniture and straightening the knick-knacks. An immaculate housekeeper, she abhorred even a hint of dirt. The Brusselmans' apartment always picked up dust that blew in from the streets. While Ann didn't like what the draft brought in, their second-story location had proven excellent for their secret work. From the terrace, the Brusselmans could see up and down Rue d'Ixelles, giving them a complete survey of the movement of the old electricity-driven streetcars. If the Germans made a mad dash up the boulevard, the Brusselman family could spot them coming from blocks away. Julien's office with the gas company downstairs on the ground floor proved equally excellent. The closeness of their home and work arrangements made the Rue d'Ixelles Street location perfect for the underground's purposes.

Ann picked up the photograph of her father, dusted it, and studied the face for a moment. Papa Ansel would never have approved of the work they were doing. He would have shouted protests and shaken his finger in the air. Papa would have warned them of the infinitely dangerous work confronting them every day. Then with his arms folded over his chest and shaking his head, he would have concluded that they could not allow those warmongering Germans to control them. Throwing both hands in the air, Papa Ansel would have walked away proclaiming, "We must do what we must do!"

The truth was, Ann's father would have been proud of their work. He simply loved his daughter too much to tell her to stick her neck out. And that was exactly what she and Julien had done. By joining the French-Belgium underground, they had enlisted in an escape organization with the capacity to plunge them into such fierce resistance that both Ann and Julien, along with their children, could end up being executed by the Gestapo at a moment's notice. Ann knew this truth well.

Placing the picture back on the shelf, Ann forced herself to stop thinking about the precarious position they had chosen to live with. She couldn't let her mind wander off without going down the road that led to paralyzing fear. The results of such a trip always proved far, far too costly for her well-being.

The phone suddenly rang. Ann jumped. Unexpected phone calls frightened her because it could be a warning that the Brusselmans had been discovered. With a trembling hand, she slowly lifted the receiver.

"Yes," Ann answered in a hesitant voice that sounded more like a question than a statement.

"I am speaking with *Frau* Brusselman?" a young man's voice said.

"*Frau*" was the tipoff that the underground was calling. Her shoulders relaxed in relief. At least, the Gestapo wasn't after them for the time being.

"Yes, this is *Frau.*"

"Good!" the familiar voice said. "I need to speak with you for a few moments."

Ann recognized Dirk Vogel's voice. Probably he was at their family farm. Usually such unexpected calls meant that

Allied soldiers were on the run and someone had landed at the Vogels' house. She would not mention any names in case the Germans were listening on some sort of telephone device, but Ann needed to clarify it was indeed Dirk.

"Your mother and father are fine?" Ann asked.

The phone went silent for far longer than normal. "My father is no longer with us," Dirk said with a distant, strained voice. "He is gone now."

Instantly Ann recognized the meaning. "O-o-h!" she gulped. "He will not be coming back?"

"No."

"I'm so sorry to hear that," Ann's voice cracked. "Do you understand?"

"Yes," the voice quivered.

Ann caught her breath and tried to quiet her heart that had started beating fast. She needed to say something but nothing appropriate came to mind.

"I must ask you a favor," the voice said. "I have two puppies that I can no longer keep under these difficult circumstances. Would there be any possibility of your taking care of them for me?"

"Of course. We'd be delighted to help."

"And I was wondering if you could come out and pick them up?"

"At your farm?" Ann knew she needed more specific direction.

"Yes, in our vicinity. I can meet you at the usual spot."

Ann knew exactly where he meant. "Spot" identified an old familiar location.

"Certainly. Would it help if I came tomorrow morning?"

"I would prefer that time. Yes, we will be waiting. I must tell you that one of the puppies has damaged his paw and will need help in getting around. Will his condition prove to be a problem?"

"We will adjust," Ann said.

"Thank you," the voice said. "I will see you at nine o'clock tomorrow and I can share . . . what happened."

"Good day," Ann said and hung up. She shook her head. "God, help them!" she gasped. "Something terrible has happened."

The noise from some distant motor kicked in a steady disconcerting drone that left an unsettling syncopation in the background. Out of nowhere the rumble of a crackling fury sailed past. Flames began to explode a wall of fire that engulfed the entire scene, filling the room with heat, burning debris, and billowing black smoke. The intensity of the fumes increased, making it impossible to breathe. Coughing broke out with such a roar that the hacking became deafening. In an instant the furnace exploded, impelling rubble and wreckage across the black sky.

Hurtling toward the earth with unceasing pain rushing across his entire body, he knew death couldn't be avoided.

Excruciating agony made him feel as if he were being roasted on a barbecue skewer. The intensity of the torture increased until the torment was no longer bearable. At that instant bullets started flying from every direction. Men with pitchforks charged out of trees, jabbing and stabbing as they lunged forward. Dogs leaped out of the bushes, excited by the scent of smoldering flesh, preparing to rip him to pieces.

His torture had become so great that dying was preferable to living. Surely death would descend in any instant. He could stand it no longer and screamed like a man being dropped into the depths of hell.

"Stop it!" Hank Holt shook the sleeping Jack Martin to silence the screaming. "Knock off the noise."

When Jack came out of his dream fog, he was still yelling. With sweat running down his face, the airman's eyes darted back and forth across the darkness in wild, frenzied fear. Only Holt's shaking him made Jack realize he was wailing so loudly that someone outside the cellar might hear him.

"I thought they ... the Germans ... were killing me," Jack said. "I guess ... I've been dreaming."

"Jack! We're still in the night. It's starting to get light outside, but if the Germans were searching for us around the farm house, they would have heard you."

Jack pushed himself up on his elbows and tried to catch his breath. He could feel his heart pounding. "I—I don't know what happened."

"Your dreams went wild."

"I thought I was dying." Jack's chest heaved up and down.

"You've got to get hold of yourself, man. Another scream like that last one could put us out of business. You're placing the Vogel family at jeopardy as well. They've already had enough tragedy."

"Yeah."

Jack dropped back on the quilt separating him from the dirt behind the cellar wall. The burning sensation in his legs seemed to have gotten worse, racking his entire body with torment. For the first time since he tried to escape from the crashing airplane, Jack Martin realized how close he had come to dying. Fear burned the specter of death into his mind and he couldn't control the images that emerged out of nowhere. For the first time in his life, Jack had looked death in the eye. The reflection proved terrifying.

God, help me, Jack Martin prayed silently. *I don't want to die.* He took a deep breath. *I'm tired of hurting, of agonizing. Please, please help me survive.*

CHAPTER SEVEN

The best highway from Brussels to Maastrich was through Liège and then north along the Albert Canal, but the Germans usually guarded that area more heavily. Ann Brusselman knew she was more likely to avoid a sudden inspection if she traveled the backwoods roads through Tienen and Tongeren. While the thoroughfare was narrow, the road was actually more direct. If she didn't get caught in farm traffic dropping her fast pace to horse speed, she would make good time. Of course, nothing was predictable since the war had started, and she could end up in a jam that might take hours. Months ago the Brusselmans learned no one could do anything about the unpredictable situation when the *Wehrmacht*, the German Army, put the heavy heel of their hobnailed boots down.

An evangelical Christian, Ann Brusselman used these unpredictable trips as a time to pray and work on Scripture memory. The Dutch Reformed Church encouraged members to commit as much of the Bible to mind as possible. "Thy

Word have I hid in my heart," had become their text for every day. Before the fighting broke out, the Brusselmans hadn't paid much attention to the pastor's admonitions to memorize Scripture. The unexpected attack of the Nazis changed everything. Abruptly they realized keeping a few Bible passages in mind made all the difference in the world.

Early on, Ann had memorized, "So have no fear of them, for nothing is covered that will not be revealed, or hidden that will not be known." After studying the passage in the book of Matthew, Ann added another verse to her memory bank. "And do not fear those who kill the body but cannot kill the soul; rather fear him who can destroy both soul and body in hell." She always reviewed those two verses while driving through the zones where the Nazis could be lurking.

Ann didn't have an easy time pushing apprehension away. The truth was that she tended to be completely undone by sudden surges of anxiety that could flash out of nowhere. Fear continually lingered in the shadows. At such times, when her apprehensions exploded, Ann turned to her Bible verses to quiet the qualms rattling around in her mind.

Ann glanced at her watch. She was making good time and should be near Maastrich soon. She hadn't seen any German vehicles and that reassured her. Maybe she could make it through without having a car check. At least, she hoped so.

Slowing the vehicle, Ann recognized the little town of St. Truiden just ahead. Villagers would be out on the streets and she needed to drive carefully. A flock of geese could come waddling out of nowhere, and that was trouble if her car came roaring through too fast. She watched carefully at the crossroads that ran up to Nieuwerken and then proceeded on to Borgloon. The coast remained clear.

The Brusselmans had been drawn into underground work through the influence of the same preacher who had dramatically influenced young Dirk Vogel. While most people thought of Pastor Harold Assink as only a village minister, the truth was that Assink's influence in fighting the Germans turned out to be extensive across Belgium. His preaching was certainly forceful enough, but it was his coordination of the French, Belgians, and Dutch that had proven to be decisive for the Brusselmans' work.

One evening Ann and Julien were sitting in their living room when someone unexpectedly knocked on their door. To their surprise they found a tall Dutchman waiting outside.

"I'm the Reverend Harold Assink," the thin pastor had said. "I happened to be in your area visiting folks and would like to get acquainted." He didn't smile. "Perhaps, I might have something that might interest you." He had stared with an intensity that seemed to shout that they should read between the lines of what he was saying.

"Come in, pastor," Julien reluctantly said.

Carrying his thick Bible as if it were Assink's badge of authority, the minister walked in and sat down with an erect, proper posture. For the first time, he smiled. "I've been checking your street. Your apartment on 127 Rue d'Ixelles is a marvelous location. Certainly you can see a long way from this second floor."

Julien and Ann looked at each in complete mystification with no idea what this minister was talking about.

"I've also discovered from your neighbors that you're patriotic Belgian citizens." Sternness returned to Assink's face. "You're *not sympathetic* with the Nazis."

Julien frowned. "You're asking dangerous questions."

"I've come about a dangerous job. We need the help of people like yourselves." Reverend Assink had leaned forward. "I believe what I need you to do *is the work of God.*"

Ann studied Harold Assink's hair. The man was obviously Dutch, but who knew what such a blunt and forward approach was really all about? Maybe he was a patriot; maybe he was a traitor. She had no idea what the tall, skinny Dutchman's purpose truly was. During a fierce war, no one could be trusted.

It had taken the Brusselmans a couple of weeks to verify that Assink was genuine, and they had to make up their minds to put themselves in jeopardy. Julien was always willing to do clandestine work. His hesitation came from a fear of putting Ann and the children at risk. The matter had been settled a week later when they received a second unexpected knock on their door. Reverend Assink had returned.

"I need to talk to you *now*," the minister had said without even exchanging a greeting and walked in.

Julien shut the door behind them. Looking directly at Ann, he raised an eyebrow.

"My dear, I understand that you speak excellent English," Assink had said with a slight British accent.

"Yes," Ann answered in English.

"Good!" Assink beamed. "I will bring you a radio you will need to hide. We must have an English speaker to translate the BBC News reports into French for our Belgian patriots. We want our people to be alert."

"I see," Ann said slowly. "Yes, I can do this task for the underground."

"Excellent!" Assink beamed like a switched-on lightbulb. "Most excellent! I will arrange for the radio to be brought in immediately. A repair man will show up tomorrow to fix something or other. He will bring the wireless in with him."

Assink started shaking hands with Julien and then stopped. "Oh, yes! Have you decided yet to allow us to use your apartment as a halfway house for smuggling Allied soldiers out of Belgium?"

Julien looked at Ann with bewilderment in his eyes.

"Yes," Ann answered for both of them. "We can do this work for the underground."

"Ah! It is a blessed thing that I hear!" Assink started another round of handshaking. "Well, I must be on my way. Remember that the Lord promised us, 'Behold, I am with you always, to the end of the age.'" With that comment, the lanky Dutchman disappeared out the front door and was gone.

Her agreement had come so quickly, Ann wasn't sure whether the decision was God, Assink's forceful personality, a quirk of fate, or a decision they should have thought about longer. The Brusselmans weren't the Calvinists that Dirk Vogel's family were, but they had heard enough forceful preaching to decide the matter must have been the will of God. At least, that's where they left the question that night when they went to bed.

Ann Brusselman slowed down well before she reached the outskirts of Maastrich to make sure she did nothing that would attract attention. Crossing the German border during these hard days was walking into the devil's lair. This aggressive, hostile country certainly wasn't Ann's fatherland. Driving inside Germany made her even more tense than usual.

Ann had always thought Maastrich to be an attractive town. The municipality was much like Belgian cities where buildings were pushed next to each other with no space in between. Tall, skinny houses with second- and third-story bedrooms appeared squeezed together like tightly bound boxes.

Ann shifted into second gear to get down the narrow streets that had originally been built only for horses. Small cars had to maneuver around each other to get through the limited space. Ahead of Ann's car, the overpowering steeple of the Roman Catholic church overshadowed everything around it. Increasing traffic brought her nearly to a stop. She needed to skirt the town square in order to get through faster.

Ann abruptly turned the corner in front of her, hoping to find a faster way back out of the city toward the little village of Tijden as well as the Vogel's farm. A German corporal abruptly stepped in front of her car with his rifle pointed at her face. Wearing the usual *Wehrmacht* uniform with the high collar and steel helmet that came over the man's ears, the soldier looked fierce and unyielding.

"*Stoppen!*" the corporal barked. "*Halten!*"

Ann slammed on the brakes and gripped the steering wheel tenaciously. "Therefore do not fear them," she quoted the Bible verse under her breath. Could the Gestapo have listened in on her phone call with Dirk? Had these Nazi soldiers been posted around the town to catch her? Ann thought she might faint.

"*Sprechen sie Deutsch?*" The soldier kept his rifle pointed at Ann's face.

"*Nein.*" Ann understood German, but she wasn't going to let this soldier know.

The corporal nodded and motioned for her to get out of the car. He jotted down her Belgian license plate number.

Leaving her purse on the seat, Ann stepped out. Because she was shaking, she held to the door for support. Immediately, another soldier appeared on the other side of the car. The two men began searching the front and back seats. Although they said nothing, their eyes caught every detail of what was in the car.

Keeping her eyes open, Ann prayed silently. "*Oh Lord, I know we are blessed when men revile and persecute us. Our reward in heaven is great. It's just that I certainly don't want to collect it right now! Please help me get through this check without going into a panic. Amen.*"

Ann had intentionally left the trunk unlocked in case she was stopped. The soldiers opened the lid and checked the area thoroughly. Finally the corporal got down on his knees and looked under the chassis. Satisfied, he nodded to the other man and turned back to Ann.

"*Erlaubnis sich Verabschieden,*" the corporal snapped and gestured for her to leave.

Ann quickly slipped back in the car, her heart pounding so hard she could barely think. Only then did she see the "One-Way" sign hammered into the brick wall. She had turned down the wrong direction into an alley! One thing was for sure. She wouldn't be coming back through Maastrich with her passengers!

"Thank You, Lord!" Ann wanted to shout but kept the car's speed down to a snail's pace. Over and over in a whisper, she kept praying, "Thank You, Lord! Thank You, Lord!"

The car headed back through the suburbs and turned south. Alongside the road the wide Sambre Meuse River rolled down toward the Albert Canal. Once she crossed the German border, Ann would turn off the main highway and wind her way through farmland to the Vogels' farm. She had been to the farm a number of times and had carefully memorized the roads. No mistakes were permitted on these passenger pick-ups. The danger remained too great.

Like most farm roads, the dirt route proved to be almost more like a trail with deep ruts. She would have a difficult time when the rains came. A cart or big-wheeled wagon would do far, far better. Finally, she crossed the narrow bridge over a small creek and recognized the long stone fence running alongside the road in front of her. Following Dirk Vogel's instructions, Ann drove down the fence line until she came to the corner where the stone fence turned abruptly to the left. Pulling up next to the wall of gray stones carefully wedged together, Ann turned off the engine. In the distance she could see the Vogels' farm. Dirk Vogel would appear only after a significant amount of time passed. The delay had been their agreed upon procedure.

Ann watched the cows grazing contentedly across the lush green fall pasture. The tranquil scene looked more like one of Claude Monet's paintings than a battlefield where at any moment antagonists might emerge from behind the trees with guns cocked and ready to kill each other. With her car windows rolled down, Ann might well have drifted off into a peaceful slumber, but "might have" didn't cover the fact that her heart kept pounding with fear that a truckload of German soldiers could show up at any minute. Nothing could cover the fact that poor Groot Vogel had been killed only days earlier.

After forty-five minutes, a head of tousled blonde hair slowly emerged above the rock wall. "P-s-s-t!" Dirk Vogel hissed.

Ann jumped. "Dirk?"

"I'm behind the stone fence," the Dutch boy said. "Do you see anyone up and down the road?"

Ann looked again. "No," she said more forcefully. "No one has been around here since I arrived."

"Good," Dirk said. "We haven't seen anyone all day either. I think we are safe."

"You have the Allied soldiers with you?"

"Yes. I don't want them to come out until you're ready to put them in your car. The injured soldier must be placed carefully in your backseat."

Ann hopped out of the car. "I'm opening the door to the backseat right now. We can move the man immediately."

Dirk Vogel stood up with Hank Holt at his side. The two men lifted Jack Martin up slowly. Holt and Martin had changed into the clothing of farm workers and looked like hired hands who worked the fields.

Jack held tightly to the rock ledge running along the top of the long fence. The two men helped him slip over the wall and drop down on the other side. With Hank Holt's shoulder under his arm, Jack staggered to the car and slumped into the backseat. The other two men hurried around and jumped in the car. Dirk quickly introduced the soldiers and then slid down in the seat to hide beside Ann.

"What happened to your father?" Ann asked immediately.

"The Nazis shot him," Dirk's voice quivered. "I think they were trying to spread fear. They also killed a British pilot in our front yard. During the shooting, these two soldiers were hiding in our basement. I was in town when all of this happened."

"I'm so, so sorry." Ann squeezed his hand. "And your poor mother?"

"She sits by the window and weeps all day long. Nothing

will be easy for her." Tears abruptly welled up in Dirk's eyes. He wiped his cheeks. "We must get you on your way at once. The two Americans must be smuggled out of the country as fast as possible. While you keep them, I will make arrangements with the underground and set up the escape route."

"Of course." For the first time Ann turned around in her seat and looked at Jack Martin's face. The American lay slumped back against the seat with his eyes closed and beads of sweat popping up on his forehead. The man looked like he was almost ready to drift off forever.

"Your friend's *really* hurting." Ann pointed over her shoulder.

"Jack got severely burned when his bomber was shot down," Dirk explained. "He needs medical attention. Can you come up with something?"

"I suppose I have to because the man is in pain," Ann shrugged. "Don't worry. We'll make sure he receives treatment."

"Good!" Dirk bit his lip. "I must get back to my mother."

Ann patted the side of his face. "You poor, poor boy. What will you ever do now that your father is gone?"

Dirk nodded his head resolutely. "I will fight all the harder. These murdering dogs will not frighten me from resisting them. We must go on until the victory is ours."

Ann squeezed his hand again. "You are a brave young man, Dirk. The future of our country rests on the shoulders of men like you. Don't worry. God is with us."

Dirk rubbed his forehead nervously. "That one fact is my hope, the only hope I have left." He forced a smile. "God bless you, Ann." Dirk opened the door quickly and hurried out of the car. With a single hop, he leaped the stone wall and disappeared into the meadow.

CHAPTER EIGHT

Gestapo leader Arnwolf Mandel kept a mistress in Brussels.

The Belgium city was far enough away from Maastrich to allow Mandel to carry on Gestapo business in Germany without any appearance of impropriety. Having a mistress was not unusual, but Arnwolf was an absolute stickler for correct appearance when it came to protecting his reputation with the secret police. Mandel had always been a man of contradictions, but none were more glaring than the contradiction between his public and private worlds.

The Mandel family had been Roman Catholics forever, living in Waldviertel, a rural area in Austria and not far from the Czechoslovakian border. The only distinction of the remote area was that Adolph Hitler's parents had been born there. As a child, Arnwolf lived through the terrible depression that devaluated German currency as well as created an apprehension about a possible takeover by the Bolsheviks that still haunted Germany. A lower-class working family, the

Mandels had exposed Arnwolf to the finer things in life but without any ability to buy them. He had grown up in an environment of "look but don't touch," watching only from considerable distance. Consequently, young Mandel developed an inordinate taste for what he could never afford. By the time he reached adolescence, the young boy had a burning desire to propel himself into a far more affluent world. He would do *anything* to succeed.

While talking a fierce story, Arnwolf had always been on the decidedly cowardly side. Attacked by a dog at five years of age, the animal left nasty puncture wounds on his legs and a pattern in his mind. He feared dogs; he wanted to kill dogs.

Adding to Arnwolf's muddle had been his strange mother, Marian. Appearing to be a gentle, passive soul, Marian seemed to enjoy havoc and always looked the other way when Johann Mandel, Arnwolf's father, beat the living daylights out of the boy. Johann tended to fly into a frenzy once he started paddling his children with a leather belt. As Arnwolf grew into a young man, several times he had gotten into fistfights with his father that ended in significant rage. The result helped shape young Arnwolf's personality in an unexpected way. His tenacious dread of injury ended up being masked by a vicious temperament. He feared his father; he wanted to kill his father.

Arnwolf Mandel remained overwhelmingly frightened of being hurt while being strangely fascinated with violence. After police training and instruction in the use of weapons, Arnwolf demonstrated a calculating ability to kill without batting an eye as long as the victim was not dominating him. Arnwolf feared his victims; he wanted to kill his victims.

Years earlier his carpenter father had been instantly enamored with Adolph Hitler after hearing the rising politician speak at a rally in Munich. The entire family had attended Nazi gatherings in the Zeppelin field in Nuremberg where they screamed and cheered as multitudes of soldiers carrying banners and flags marched into the vast stadium. Along with the mob of workers like themselves, the Mandel family frantically believed Hitler would prove to be their answer in the quest for a better life. By 1943, the fall of every country around them from Poland to the Netherlands seemed to guarantee wealth would soon flow through their front door.

In the late '30s, Arnwolf seized the opportunity to enter the Gestapo and had risen rapidly through the ranks. His dress predictably looked crisp and sharp like any rising young man should appear. At the same time, both his business office and apartment remained the height of confusion and chaos.

Arnwolf filled his home and office with junk piled on top of junk. He didn't have the ability to keep anything in an orderly manner. His habit of throwing used clothing on chairs or hanging pants on a door went unchecked. Dirty coffee cups sat for days on stained doilies. Unread books sat on top of books, and heaping waste paper baskets stayed unemptied. His public appearance and the way he lived were from two different planets.

Arnwolf walked quickly down the hall of the Brussels apartment building. Unlocking and then shutting the door to Arabella Kersten's apartment behind him, Arnwolf strolled in with the cavalier swagger he always had when he secretly entered his mistress's private boudoir.

"Arnwolf!" Arabella looked up from her dressing table where she was brushing her hair and wearing only a silk house robe. "You are early."

"Caught you unprepared?" Arnwolf said with a slight inflection that sounded both playful and hinted at possible unfaithfulness to him.

"I am never unprepared for my heartthrob." She let the robe slide open, extending her bare leg forward. "Give your little sugar a kiss." She beckoned for him.

Arnwolf looked at her coldly. Arabella was a pretty thing with long blonde hair combed over her shoulders. Brilliant blue eyes accented her attractive face, and she certainly had a full, striking figure. Yet, the truth was that he felt nothing for her. Like himself, she had come from a poor family and was trying to scratch her way up to a higher place in society. Her sweet words never revealed her heart.

Walking across the room with his usual swagger, he leaned over and gave her a simple kiss on the cheek.

"Come on, baby." Arabella batted her eyes. "Show me some passion." She grinned but didn't stop talking. "And what have you been doing today?" The woman winked. "I bet my little sweetie has been out there on the hot road running down all the enemies of the Fatherland? Tell me exactly where you've been and what you've done. Hmm?"

Arnwolf knew that once this woman rolled into her endless questions, she'd babble on and on like a broken record. Her incessant, constant schmoozing into every corner of his life drove him nuts. His visits were for one thing only, and the never-ending mouth machine pushed him over the edge.

"And what did my little flame find for me?"

Arnwolf grabbed the back of her neck and kissed Arabella so passionately she couldn't speak. At first she squirmed, then grabbed his shoulders, but finally pushed him away.

"That hurt!" she complained.

Arnwolf grinned.

The return trip from the Vogel farm had not been as arduous as Ann Brusselman feared. To avoid going back to Maastrich, Madame Brusselman had taken the highway to Liège and then turned west to Brussels. Thick, dark clouds hung low in the sky. The two American men she had picked up said little.

"Who's this woman?" Jack Martin said in a hushed voice.

"Don't know," Hank Holt answered. "We'll see in time."

Because she and Dirk Vogel spoke in Dutch, the Americans obviously assumed she did not understand English. To the contrary, Ann understood everything they said to each other.

"How are you doing?" Hank Holt asked his friend.

Ann watched in her rearview mirror as the man resting in the backseat kept his eyes closed. He rubbed his forehead and opened his eyes slowly.

"N-not well," Jack mumbled.

"I don't know how much longer it will be until we stop," Holt said. "But hang on. We're making good time."

"We are not far from Brussels," Ann suddenly interjected in excellent English with a British accent. "We should be there in approximately thirty minutes."

"Oh!" Hank Holt blinked several times. "I didn't realize you spoke our language so well."

"One must learn to speak many languages when living in Belgium," Ann explained. "Many do."

Jack pushed himself up in the seat and rubbed his forehead. "I'm not feeling so great today."

"Your legs are the problem?" Ann asked.

"Afraid so," Jack said slowly. "Got a nasty burn."

"So I understand," Ann said. "I'm going to see if we can get some medical care."

"Good." Jack closed his eyes and leaned his head back against the seat.

"Where we going?" Hank asked. "I've got no idea what's happening."

"Have you ever heard of the Comete Line?" Ann glanced in the mirror to read the look on the man's face.

Hank frowned. "No, no. Never heard of it."

"Do you know anything about the French-Belgian underground resistance organizations?"

Hank shook his head. "Sorry. I never expected to sit down around here until after the Nazis were long gone." He grinned.

Ann liked the man's face. His responses seemed open, honest, straightforward—and that was the key. No one could afford the possibility of a spy worming his way into their organization. The stakes were far too high.

"No, ma'am," Hank said. "I'm afraid I have no idea what you are talking about."

Ann watched Jack Martin's face. He had already closed his eyes and seemed almost out of it. She didn't need to worry about these two men's validity.

"The Comete Line is your secret road to an escape," Ann began. "We are patriotic citizens who do everything we can to resist the Nazis. Our mission is to help Allied soldiers who are trapped behind the German lines get out of the country."

"Wow!" Hank said. "That's a noble cause. How can we ever thank you for daring to help us?"

"Just escape," Ann said. "You must remember our job is far from done. Never forget that the Gestapo and the German Army is everywhere. Nazis are not going to let you out of the country if they can help it. We have a dangerous road in front of us and must be careful."

"Yes," Hank said thoughtfully. "No question about it. This won't be an easy path to walk."

"W-walk?" Jack moaned. "I hoped we could thumb a ride."

Hank laughed. "Jack jokes around even when he's hurting," he explained. "We're just ole American flyboys who—"

The sudden roar of an airplane swooping down on them silenced all conversation. The fighter shot over the top of the car and soared back into the sky.

"They're trying to hit us!" Hank shouted.

"No," Ann said. "I think probably at least two airplanes are locked in a battle. We just happen to be at this spot on the highway."

"A dogfight!" Hank shouted.

Jack sat straight up in the seat. His bloodshot eyes popped open. "God, help us! They're attacking again."

"Hang on!" Ann swerved the car sharply to the right. "We've got to get off this road before we get accidentally hit. We need a shelter!"

"Up there!" Hank leaned over the seat and pointed straight ahead. "There's a bridge we can hide under if we can get there fast enough and squeeze underneath it."

Without turning back onto the highway, Ann drove down the ditch. The car bounced like it was totally out of control. Jack groaned and grabbed his legs.

"Hang on tight!" Ann shouted. "We're going on a rough ride. Careful back there!"

The vehicle kept lurching back and forth, but Ann maneuvered the careening car until she pulled under the old wooden bridge and came to an abrupt stop. She shut the engine off.

"Get down!" Ann commanded. "Get your heads down."

The roar of another airplane thundered over the bridge. Ann looked out the window cautiously and watched the sky for a moment.

"Looks like a German Messerschmitt is chasing an Allied P-40 fighter plane," Ann said. "There's a fierce fight going on over our heads."

"That's our boys!" Jack exclaimed.

An airplane rumbled above them. Suddenly the sound of bullets ripping into the bridge exploded overhead. One of the airplane's machine gun bullets broke through the wooden planks and cracked through the side of the top of the car. Ann grabbed her head and tried to roll under the steering wheel.

"Something's happened!" Hank hollered from the backseat. "Listen to that sound. It's like a bomb dropping."

The high-pitched whine of a projectile falling out of the sky grew in intensity. The increasing stridency sounded like a bomb was hurtling down on top of them.

"God, help us!" Ann prayed.

The ground shook. Ann's car bounced sideways. A roar of smoke and flames swept across the field not far away. As abruptly as the explosion began, quiet settled around them again. All Ann could hear was the crackling noise of something burning. She poked her head up and looked.

Pieces of an airplane were scattered around not more than a hundred yards from the bridge. One of the airplanes had crashed straight into the field. Smoke started drifting over the car. The explosion had been so great that Ann couldn't identify even the country of the airplane.

"We've got to get out of here!" Ann immediately turned the car engine back on. "Somebody could come roaring in here fast. Probably the German Army's already on the road. We can't wait to find out who shows up."

"Yeah," Jack agreed. "The Krauts came after us before my parachute even hit the ground when we crashed."

Ann roared up the side of the embankment and bounced over the shoulder. She flew back onto the highway. In a matter of moments, Ann had pushed the small car to its maximum speed. Hanging onto the steering wheel with fierce intensity, she headed straight for Brussels.

"Could have killed us," Ann mumbled under her breath. "I swear! Nowhere's safe anymore these days."

CHAPTER NINE

Madame Ann Brusselman drove her car around to the back alley and parked behind the tall building where her and Julien's apartment faced Rue d'Ixelles Street. Trying to look innocuous, the American pilots stayed slouched down in the backseat. With painful slowness, Ann and Hank Holt helped Jack Martin out of the car and into the rear entrance, guiding him slowly up the back stairs. The trip proved to be arduous. Ann could only hope no one was watching them.

Halfway up the wooden flight of stairs, Jack grabbed the handrail and hung on fiercely. Sweat trickled down from his forehead and his arms shook. To keep from falling, he slumped against the wall.

"Got to rest," Jack groaned. "Pain's eating me up."

"We can't stop," Ann said. "If someone sees us, we're in trouble.

Jack nodded. "I know." He gritted his teeth. "I'm not sure I can make it. Maybe, you'd better go on without me."

"Yes, you can!" Hank insisted. "Come on, Jack. We've got to move it up these stairs."

With fierce determination, Jack grabbed the rail with both hands. "Moving my legs upwards is killing me."

"Get under his arms," Ann snapped. "I'll get one side and you get on the other. We'll have to carry him up the stairs."

"You can't do that," Hank protested. "Jack weighs nearly one hundred and eighty-five pounds."

"Get moving," Ann demanded. "Time is running out."

Pushing with everything in her, Ann slowly staggered up the steps. Holt maintained a steady march from the other side. When they reached the second floor, Martin completely slumped, but Ann and Hank kept walking until they reached the back door to the Brusselmans' apartment. Ann quickly unlocked the door and they hustled Jack inside. Without stopping, Ann led them into her and Julien's bedroom. With careful, slow motions, they laid Jack on the bed. He instantly passed out. Ann rushed to the telephone.

"Please give me Dr. Gaetan," Ann told the nurse. "I have an *unexpected* emergency."

"Immediately," the nurse answered.

The phrase *unexpected emergency* was obviously a coded message to warn both the nurse and the doctor that the situation was a problem arising from the underground's work. Those words always got immediate response. In a couple of minutes, Dr. Gaetan was on the line.

"I understand we have a problem," Gaetan began professionally.

"Definitely," Ann said. "How soon could you come?"

"Where?"

"My *usual* place."

"And the problem?" Dr. Gaetan pressed.

"Burns. Severe burns."

"I see," the doctor said slowly. "I will come prepared."

"Urgency is required."

"I'll be there in twenty minutes." The doctor hung up.

Ann replaced the phone slowly and turned to Hank. "We must have this man ready for examination the second the doctor arrives. I will get a blanket to put under his legs. Please remove his pants and get him ready for the doctor."

"Sure," Hank said. "Jack's passed out, but I'll be careful. I sure hope the doctor can do something."

Ann nodded and hurried out of the room. In a hall linen closet, she found a cotton blanket that could be slipped under the pilot's legs. Ann had never seen severe burns before and had no idea of what to expect. Pulling the blanket out and slipping it over her arm, Ann scurried back to the bedroom, but when she reached the door, Ann stopped and stared. She caught her breath.

Jack Martin's legs looked like they'd been roasted over an open fire. His skin had peeled back, revealing the raw red tissue underneath. Black scabs of severely burned epidermis had curled up on the front. The tops of his feet were badly burned, but not as drastically as the shins and calves of his legs. The sight made her want to gag.

"God, help us!" Ann half prayed aloud. "He's in serious trouble."

"Yeah," Hank said. "I hope this doc knows what he's doing."

"Dr. Gaetan is excellent. If he can't fix him, nobody can."

Hank looked up at her slowly with a hesitation in his eyes that asked the question his mouth wouldn't say. Ann read it clearly. "*Can anyone really help Jack Martin?*"

When Dr. Gaetan arrived as quickly as he promised, Madame Brusselman immediately ushered him back to the bedroom where Hank stood beside the bed. Martin's eyes remained closed. A tall, distinguished man with white hair and small glasses perched on his nose, the doctor wore a professional suit that left a no-nonsense impression. For a few moments, the doctor studied the patient before setting his black bag on the bed. He rubbed his chin thoughtfully and then turned to Ann.

"This man has been most seriously injured," Dr. Gaetan began in French. "Much of the burned area is third degree, and many men die from injuries that are this significant. Unfortunately, we are not able to give him intravenous fluids in this setting. The task is most serious. For this sort of burn, we have a procedure that is unfortunately necessary." He opened the bag and shook his head. "Frankly, I am not sure there is anything that I can do to help much." He took out instruments wrapped in a flannel cloth holder and laid them on the bed. "Very serious problem," he mumbled to himself.

"What can we do?" Ann asked.

"The man must not scream," Gaetan explained. "Security always remains a serious problem in this building as you well know."

"Scream?" Ann shuddered.

"The first procedure I must use is called eschar." The doctor raised an eyebrow. "It is necessary that I scrape away the dead skin and destroyed areas. Obviously, such a procedure with a scalpel is extraordinarily painful."

Ann closed her eyes for a moment and caught her breath again. "Bloody, I suppose?"

The doctor nodded his head. "We must tie this man's hands and body to the bed as well as put a gag in his mouth to keep him from making unexpected noise. I will give him a shot of morphine before we begin. Do you have any rope?"

"No." Ann shook her head. "We could tear up some sheets and tie him with the cloth."

"Let's do it as quickly as possible," the doctor said and picked up a syringe. "I'll give him a sedative with morphine before you start. You will need to boil several towels while I am doing these things."

Ann nodded and motioned for Hank to follow her. Out in the hall, she quickly explained in English what was about to happen. Holt shook his head and frowned.

"Doesn't sound good," Hank said.

"I want you to stand by his head," Ann continued. "If he starts to scream, you must hold a towel over his mouth. Understand?"

Hank nodded. "Yeah, I got ya." He rubbed his hands together nervously. "I guess we've got no choice."

"Exactly," Ann said. "Now, I'm going to get the sheets to tie him down. You go back in there and help in anyway you can."

Hank bit his lip and went back into the room. Ann returned to the hall linen closet and found an old sheet they could tear apart. She paused long enough to rip off a number of long strips. Grabbing four towels, Ann hurried into the kitchen to boil a couple of the towels in a large pot over her kitchen stove. She knew it would take several minutes to get them hot enough. Only after the boiling water had sterilized the towels did Ann return to the bedroom.

Saying nothing, Ann laid the steaming towels in a pan on the bed beside Jack's legs and handed Hank several strips of the old sheet. She immediately started tying Jack's arms to the bed. Hank did the same thing on the other side. Once several other strips had been tied around Jack's middle, Ann tied a gag around his mouth. Hank made one final run with a cloth strip to lock Jack's thighs to the bed. Martin didn't make a sound and seemed to be completely unconscious. While they worked, the doctor kept unfolding instruments and laying out gauze near the hot towels Ann had brought in. Ann pressed a dry towel into Hank's hands.

"For his face," Ann said. "Keep him from screaming."

Hank nodded soberly.

Dr. Gaetan straightened and rolled up his sleeves. "I am ready to begin," he said in English and glanced at Hank Holt with a severe look in his eyes. *"Get ready!"*

Hank dropped down on one knee by the bedside and got hold of Jack's shoulders. "Hang on, partner," he said in a near whisper. Jack didn't move.

The doctor bent over and began to work.

"*A-a-a-h!*" Suddenly Jack Martin came out of his stupor with a violent scream.

Hank crammed the towel into his mouth and forced him back on the bed. Jack's eyes had a wild, crazed look. The towel subdued any further screams, but the pilot writhed on the bed with closed eyes.

"Keep the towel in place," the doctor warned in English. "He will scream again."

For the next ten minutes Jack Martin wrenched back and forth while Hank Holt pressed the dry towel into his mouth. Ann watched the beads of perspiration on Jack's forehead turn into trickles and then streams of sweat that ran down the side of his face. Periodically the man tried to scream, but Hank kept the towel in place.

Finally the doctor straightened up with an exasperated look on his face. "I don't think we can do any more," he said. "At least, the wounds are cleaned and the dead skin removed." Gaetan shook his head. "The pain will be great tomorrow."

"Will he make it, doctor?" Ann asked in French.

"I don't know," Gaetan shook his head and answered in French. "The problem is serious and my big concern is infection. If he gets poisoning in one of these open areas I have scraped, the man's chances are not good."

"Can't you do anything?" Ann implored.

"New drugs have come out since this war began," Dr. Gaetan continued in French. "The Americans call the medications antibiotics and say they do wonders with infection. Unfortunately, I've never tried one before now. I'm willing to attempt its usage if you agree to approve of the application."

Ann ran her hands nervously through her hair. "I'm no doctor. How would I know?"

"I don't expect you to know, but only take responsibility," Dr. Gaetan said.

"He may die anyway," Ann said slowly, "and the drug *could* help."

"Everything is a risk these days," the doctor said. "I think we must chance making mistakes."

"What's this new drug called?" Ann asked.

"Penicillin."

"Okay. Let's do it," Ann agreed.

"Madame Brusselman," the doctor said in English, "the man should be left on this bed until we see significant improvement. Further, I know prayer is controversial with some people. However, I would suggest that we all pray for this man. He is near the end of his rope."

Ann nodded. "We will pray," she answered in English. "Yes, we will start immediately." Ann turned to Hank Holt. "Are you a Christian?"

"Yes, ma'am," Hank nodded enthusiastically.

"Then this is the time to start praying."

"I-I will!" Hank said. "S-sure."

"Okay, doctor. We have done our best. How can we thank you for coming so quickly?"

"Keeping him from dying will do just fine." The doctor began putting his instruments back in the bag. "Our job is to help them survive. Some days it's easier than others." He started unrolling his sleeves. "Some days it's hard."

Arnwolf Mandel paced back and forth in his Gestapo office in Maastrich. The overweight officer kept thinking about the alternatives before him. Periodically he glanced at a large map of Belgium he had thumbtacked to the wall. Having returned from his time in Ghent with Arabella Kersten, Mandel still felt unsettled and disconcerted because he couldn't get a problem out of his mind. Matters weren't going exactly as he had hoped.

Colonel Schmidt's first phone call had opened new possibilities for Mandel beyond what he dreamed possible. Normally his agents spent their time spying on German citizens and following leads offered more by village gossip than hard facts. Most of the work was dull and went nowhere. For a man as ambitious as Mandel, villages like Margraten and Voerendaal clustered around the larger town of Maastrich offered no doors of opportunity. But Schmidt had invited him to chase Allied soldiers, and that possibility was filled with promise. *Real promise!*

Mandel reasoned that the war would not last much longer. The Americans would try to invade Europe and be slaughtered on some nameless beach in France or Belgium. Maybe in the Netherlands. They'd never get beyond Ghent or Arnhem, and then, with what was left of the wreckage of their army, their generals would sue for peace. He had to get in all the points he could *now* with the central office in Berlin and, hopefully, people like Himmler. The issue demanded immediate action and resolve. Mandel needed to take the bull by the horns and create a new situation that would put him in the best possible light. Something quick, unexpected, and significant in its return.

"Herrick!" Mandel shouted. "Come in here!"

Karl Herrick promptly hustled into the room. *"Mein herr,"* Herrick kept bowing in quick jerky movements. "At your service."

"Sit down." Mandel pointed to the chair in front of his desk. "I would like your ... a ... assistance. Your thinking." Running his hand over his plastered-down blond hair, Mandel kept pacing back and forth.

"Of course," Herrick said. "How can I help, *mein leiter?*"

"I believe the execution of Groot Vogel and the British airman we caught under Vogel's haystack created excellent propaganda for the Reich. I am sure that local citizens were impressed."

"Yes." Herrick nodded his head enthusiastically. "Definitely."

"However, we caught only one British flyboy." Mandel kept rubbing his chin thoughtfully. *"Only one."*

"Unfortunately, the two pilots from the earlier air crash are still on the run."

"Exactly," Mandel said thoughtfully. "We only have one Allied soldier that we've caught in Belgium. I don't think that the number one accomplishes our goal."

Herrick looked mystified but said nothing.

"I think we must increase our work in Belgium. After all, that is the country where the Vogels' farm is and our offices abut Belgium. I think that old farmer I killed had some sort of link with the underground." He walked across the office and thumped on a large map thumbtacked to the wall. "I believe we must analyze the Belgian countryside more completely."

Herrick nodded. "I understand. Unfortunately, our resources are somewhat limited. We would need more agents and—"

"Exactly!" Mandel cut him off. "I want you to prepare a letter to Berlin requesting they send more agents that I will personally supervise in Belgium." He tapped on the map. "Notice what town is at the end of the Albert Canal."

"Antwerp?"

"Exactly. I believe we have two centers that we must pay attention to. Antwerp and Brussels. Antwerp opens the door to the North Sea, and all roads lead to Brussels. I believe that I must survey these two cities more intently."

Karl Herrick studied the map for several moments. "In order for Berlin to justify sending you more agents, you must demonstrate a precise need. An exact count." Herrick's voice had lost the sound of intimidation that it usually carried. He spoke with more assertion and insight than usual. "I believe an exact plan of action must be developed with these objectives in mind."

Mandel's eyes narrowed. Herrick had more intelligence than the man often demonstrated. Mandel had already noticed that behind the compliant disposition lay a much more commanding personality. Today he needed Herrick's decisiveness.

"I want you to draw up such a plan," Mandel said. "Then I will make revisions and adjustments. We will propose checking and rechecking all leads until we have trapped these culprits."

"And who would be our precise targets?"

"I still want to capture those two American pilots that crashed the B-17 near the Sambre Meuse River. They may still be within our grasp."

CHAPTER TEN

During the few days that followed Dr. Gaetan's first visit, the doctor returned on a daily basis, but there was little progress. Much of the time Jack Martin appeared to be in a coma. When he was awake, the pain proved to be almost unbearable. Jack's temperature started to rise and the doctor kept giving him penicillin. No one knew what would happen. Finally on Friday afternoon, the white-haired doctor came out of the bedroom and closed the door quietly. His face conveyed the deepest concern.

"What do you think?" Ann Brusselman asked.

"Let me put it in laymen's terms," Dr. Gaetan began. "We have reached a critical point. In my experience patients usually die fairly quickly after they reach this stage. The only difference is that I am still giving him this new drug. Unless we have marked positive change quickly, I don't think this American will be here next week."

Ann wrung her hands. "There is nothing we can do but keep on praying."

"And that is no small matter." Gaetan shook his head. "I cannot come here tomorrow or on Sunday. If he dies over the weekend, you must dispose of the body."

Ann took a deep breath. "I understand."

Dr. Gaetan squeezed her hand. "God bless you, my dear." He walked out the back door of the house to go down the stairs that led to the alley.

For a few moments, Ann stood in front of the doorway to the bedroom and thought about the situation. She couldn't call any friends at their church, and contacting Rev. Harold Assink would be highly dangerous. Nothing was left except for her family to take responsibility.

"Children!" Ann called out and walked into the living room. "Children! Come into the living room."

Twelve-year-old Yvonne came into the room followed by little Jacques. Hank Holt had been sitting in the corner and put his paper down.

"Julien!" Ann called out. "Where are you?"

"In here," Julien called from the kitchen.

"Please come in the living room," Ann answered.

Wearing a towel around his waist, Julien came in with a carving knife in his hand. "What's going on?" he said. "I'm cutting up vegetables."

"Dr. Gaetan says that our patient isn't doing very well," Ann began. "In fact, Jack's in critical condition. He thinks it is very important for us to pray for him right now."

"But my teacher at catechism class said that John Calvin

didn't believe that praying for the sick helped," Yvonne inter-jected. "And I need to finish my homework that—"

"Stop it!" Ann demanded. "We all appreciate the teaching of the reformer John Calvin, but the Bible also says we should pray for the sick. Your homework can wait."

Yvonne rolled her eyes and put her hands on her hips.

"No nonsense!" Julien shook his finger at his daughter. "Praying for this sick man is the most important thing any of us has to do right now."

Hank got up out of his chair. "I don't know where Jack's condition is going," he said. "I'm sure Jack is doing his best. If praying can help, let's do it."

Yvonne nodded her head. "Yes. I guess you are right."

"I'm going to suggest that we form a circle around Jack's bed," Ann said. "I will be on one end and Julien on the other where we can hold Jack's hands. We will all join hands and pray fervently."

"Yeah," Jacques said. "I'll help too."

"Okay." Ann nodded toward the bedroom. "Let's go in and pray."

The five made a semicircle around the end of the bed, each holding the other's hand. Jack didn't move or make a sound.

Ann picked up a Bible. "I am going to read what the Scripture tells us to do." Ann turned to the book of James. "Is any one among you suffering? Let him pray. Is any cheerful? Let him sing praise. Is any among you sick? Let him call for the elders of the church, and let them pray over him, anointing him with oil in the name of the Lord." Ann stopped. "Julien, do you have any oil?"

"In the kitchen is some olive oil. Let me go get it." Julien jumped up and hurried to the kitchen. In a few moments, Julien came back into the room with a small bottle of olive oil.

"Okay, Julien," Ann said, "start by anointing this man and then we will all pray as the Bible teaches us."

Julien began mumbling a prayer under his breath while gently and carefully moistening his fingers with the oil. With his index finger, he made the sign of a cross on Jack's forehead. Each person in the family began praying softly. For fifteen minutes the intercessions continued. Finally Julien brought the prayers to a close. For several minutes they stood silently by the bed, with little Jacques sniffling.

"We shall see," Ann finally said. "Everything is now in God's hands."

They left the room and Ann closed the door behind them.

Working for the resistance offered the Brusselmans an advantage that most of the citizens of Belgium didn't have. News from across Europe, which the Nazis suppressed, came to them through the underground. These bits and pieces of information offered them insight and encouragement to keep on fighting. Madame Brusselman had already heard about the Jewish Warsaw Ghetto uprisings by the middle of June 1943.

Whispered stories described an elaborate system of tunnels, bunkers, and hideouts constructed across the Jewish ghetto that forced SS Commander Jurgen Sroop and his Nazi troops to use flame throwers, gas, and grenades to flush the Jews out. With pistols, Molotov cocktails, and a few rifles smuggled into the ghetto, the Jews had proved formidable. Clandestine reports described how poorly armed Jewish fighters with no military experience had fought back the Nazi forces using cannons and tanks until finally the Jews were overwhelmed by the sheer weight of the German war machine.

On her hidden radio Ann also heard a report from the BBC that William Temple, the Archbishop of Canterbury, had moved in the House of Lords that Britain lift all quotas for immigrating Jews. Archbishop Temple had insisted that the English must help the Jews escape persecution. Ann translated the broadcast into French and passed it along to the Comete Line underground.

From Russia surfaced the report that the Germans had failed in their attempts to take Stalingrad and many had been captured and taken prisoner. Reports said the German carnage had been horrendous. Madame Brusselman wasn't sure how to assimilate this data, but it gave her encouragement that the Nazis were struggling far more than they would ever admit publicly.

These smuggled pieces of information fortified the agents serving the Comete Line to recognize their work was vital and worthy of risking their lives. Because she feared most for her children Yvonne and Jacques, Madame Brusselman always found hearing these news reports to be personally reassuring. While she struggled to avoid thinking of what could happen to her, Ann Brusselman remained terrified of what the Gestapo would do if they caught her.

On Sunday afternoon, Madame Brusselman watched Yvonne timidly approach her while she sat knitting in a corner of the living room. Without looking up, Ann knew Yvonne was fidgeting from one foot to the other, trying to ask some difficult question. Finally, Yvonne got up enough nerve to speak.

"Ma'ma," Yvonne said. "Do you think that man in your bedroom will live?"

Startled, Ann almost answered but stopped. "Why do you ask such a question, child?"

"I've never seen a dead man." Yvonne shivered. "I feel frightened."

Ann wrapped her arms around her child's shoulders. "Oh Yvonne! You don't have to be afraid. If our friend dies, he will go to heaven and that is good." She looked into Yvonne's eyes. "Do you believe me?"

"Yes, ma'ma," replied Yvonne. "I guess I also worry about us. What if the bad soldiers come to our house?"

Ann took a deep breath. "Yvonne, our country is fighting an enemy that wants to steal our freedom, and the Nazis are killing Jewish people. We are living in a terrible time when all good people struggle to avoid being captured by these bad men. Of course, it's frightening!" Ann shook her finger like a teacher making a point in class. "But the only way we have to fight these bad men is by trying to help people like the American sleeping in our bedroom. Your father and I are glad to sleep in here on the couch at night. Now Yvonne, I do not believe the soldiers will ever come to our house, so don't worry about that."

Yvonne nodded her head. "Okay. I hope our prayers helped that soldier with his burns."

"I am sure they did," Ann said. "Don't you worry anymore. Okay?"

Ann watched apprehensively as Yvonne slowly walked away. War was terrible enough without the consequences being visited on a child. She knew the matter would not be settled only because Yvonne had received reassurance from her mother. Her daughter would keep on worrying about German maniacs breaking their door down and rushing in to grab them. It was certainly not the path either she or Julien would have chosen for their family.

Ann laid her knitting down and slowly walked across the room toward their bedroom. By this time Jack Martin's condition would probably have gotten a great deal worse. Ann knew she would have to come up with some way to remove the body without the children seeing and Julien would need to have a plan for disposing of the American. The task would be difficult.

Taking a deep breath, Ann slowly turned the doorknob and carefully pushed the door open. To her shock, Jack Martin was sitting up, leaning against the head of the bed.

"Come in," Jack said. "I'm feeling much better today."

Ann felt her mouth drop. "You're . . . you're . . . awake!"

"Yes," Jack said. "The pain's certainly there, but my fever's gone." He smiled. "Been a tough couple of days."

"More than you can imagine!" Ann's voice was barely audible. "Much more."

When Dr. Gaetan returned on Monday, the good physician was shocked by Jack Martin's improved appearance. Shaking his head, Gaetan stalked around the bedroom muttering to himself and rubbing his chin.

"Absolutely astonishing," Gaetan confided to Madame Brusselman in French. "I didn't expect him to be alive today."

Ann nodded her head. "I thought as much."

"I can't tell whether it's the new drug or the prayer." The doctor crossed his arms over his chest and pursed his lips. "Has to be both."

"*Mais oui!*" Ann said. "I think both."

Dr. Gaetan left through the back door with a perplexed look on his face and hurried down the stairs as he always did. Madame Brusselman returned to the household duties with a smile on her face. During that week Hank Holt did not leave the apartment and slept by Martin's bed at night. Jack continued to improve and by the following Sunday he was hobbling around the house, taking short steps and walking on crutches the doctor had brought in wrapped in newspaper.

Late at night, Julien and Ann talked about the next step. She had sent word to Dirk Vogel to wait on escape plans until Martin improved significantly. Regardless of Jack's struggle even to walk, the Americans had to start getting prepared for their exit out of the country. Ann Brusselman reasoned that the men must obtain French identity cards as quickly as possible. Even if someone showed up at their apartment, identity cards would answer questions. They simply had to come up with those detestable paper slips the Germans demanded to see. Julien warned Ann that she must not take these two men into downtown Brussels in their car. Driving across the country to Maastrich, Germany, was bad enough, but she couldn't chance having their car identified driving around loaded with strange men in Brussels.

After several nights of pondering the problem, Ann could see no other way out but taking the tram. Certainly, the old electric coaches would take them straight in front of the special offices where they took pictures needed for the documents. No other shop in Brussels made photos that met Nazi qualifications. Martin would have to walk on crutches, but Hank Holt could help him hobble along.

They could make the trip, but that wasn't the problem.

An unknown element in the journey rolled around in Ann's head. She could not foresee how they might manage this difficulty. The Germans had started periodically stopping trams and forcing everyone out on the street. With their rifles cocked to fire, the Nazis would march everyone up against the nearest wall and make them stand with their hands pressed behind their heads until the inspection had been completed. Ann knew if there was any identity check of papers these two men would be instantly arrested.

They could make the trip, but what if?

Ann turned restlessly in her sleep. She had no answers for such a possible crisis.

———

Ann watched Jack hobble to the breakfast table on Monday morning with a smile on his face.

"Hey!" Jack said. "I may live."

Ann stiffened and stared at the table.

"I don't think so," Hank Holt quipped. "They tell me the Krauts got your picture plastered up on the buildings. They're looking for you behind every tree."

Both men laughed, but Ann walked back to the kitchen sink and stared at the dishes. These Americans had a strange sense of humor. Maybe they understood the danger; maybe they didn't. She didn't like their joking around about what could happen.

"Gentlemen!" Ann said harshly. "We must take a trip today." She turned and faced both men like an irritated drill sergeant. "This task means leaving this house and going down the street. Germans will be everywhere."

The smiles disappeared from both men's faces. She had their total attention.

"I must remind you that we also have Gestapo agents walking around in civilian clothes watching everyone," Ann continued. "No one knows who they are or where they might be. A simple trip to the grocery store can prove harrowing."

Jack pulled at his chin. "How will I get around?"

"You will have to walk on those crutches," Ann said. "We can help you get down the stairs, but once we're on the street you'll need to walk as normally as possible. We'll put both of you back in laborers' clothing and I hope you'll blend in with the local people."

"Well," Hank said slowly, "sounds like we've got a little maneuvering to do today."

"Yeah," Jack said. "I can hardly walk. Makes me nervous."

"Nervous?" Ann bore down. "Should make you terrified."

CHAPTER ELEVEN

Getting Jack Martin down the stairs proved to be as difficult as it had been getting him up. Jack could swing his legs back and forth. Bending them proved to be overwhelmingly agonizing. Madame Brusselman got under one arm and Hank Holt the other. With careful, slow steps they maneuvered him one step at a time. Reaching the bottom, they had to stop to allow Jack to catch his breath. Perspiration dotted his forehead and he looked racked with pain.

"You okay?" Ann asked.

"Not great," Jack puffed. "But we have to do what we have to do." He reached out to steady himself against the railing.

"We can go back," Ann offered.

"I had a German grandfather," Jack said. "Name was Heinrich Matthys. Old Hennie lived with us through the Great Depression in the Thirties. When our sources of money had dried up, he'd preach to my father like an old evangelist. 'Endurance is paramount!' If I heard Grandpa say it once, I heard him say it a thousand times. You can't get there if you don't keep pushing."

"Now that we've got the sermon," Hank said. "It's time for the altar call. You ready to start walking?"

Jack bit his lip. "As ready as I'll get today."

"Let's go," Hank said.

"It's getting cold outside." Ann picked up two coats hanging on the wall. "Put these on. It'll help you look like anyone else."

Taking a deep breath, Jack started walking toward the door with his crutches swinging. His steps were short, nevertheless, he stumbled onward with his stiff-legged gait.

"The tram stops in front of our house," Ann said. "When we get outside, we'll wait by the curb but you must be ready, Jack. We will have to get on the coach as quickly as possible and it won't be easy."

Jack said nothing but kept swinging his legs stiffly forward.

Once outside, the threesome kept shuffling toward the curb. After a couple of minutes, the tram appeared up the street.

"Let's get moving," Ann said. "Walk out there ready to get on."

Saying nothing, Jack staggered forward into the brick-paved street. Ann and Hank stayed close to his side. They kept moving closer to where the tram would stop. With the clinking grind of wheels rolling over the metal rails, the old car pulled to a halt. Instantly, Ann and Hank lifted Jack up the metal steps. Gritting his teeth, the pilot said nothing but lumbered forward. Finally he reached the top step and plopped into the nearest vacant seat along the side of the car. Ann sat across from him and Hank where she had a clear view of everything happening in the coach. The tram pulled away. Ann watched Jack's eyes that were filled with pain.

Abruptly the tram stopped. A lone German soldier boarded the car, wearing a steel helmet that came down over his ears and carrying a rifle over his shoulder. The sound of his black leather boots clumping down the aisle rattled her. The man must have waved at the conductor from the street, forcing him to stop the vehicle.

Talking around the coach ceased. No one spoke to the soldier. The German looked at his fellow passengers like he wanted to speak but everyone looked away. With a look of quiet resolution he sat down five feet from Ann. Only a few seats away and on the same side sat the Americans.

Ann froze. Having a German soldier rubbing elbows with them was not her idea of a trip downtown. Every fear she had of being stopped for an identification search exploded in her mind. What would she do if this soldier was only the first and a unit of Gestapo men showed up at the next stop? Ann swallowed hard.

She would have no choice but to deny knowing Jack and Hank. If she were to escape and keep doing her underground work, Ann knew she'd flash her identity card before the soldiers's eyes and then walk away, leaving the Americans to their fate. Even the thought made her stomach flip-flop.

Ann reached for the edge of the seat and gripped it with fierce tightness.

The German smiled at her and winked. Instantly, Ann looked away as if offended. He kept looking at her but she refused to make eye contact. After several seconds, the man looked back out the window.

Jack Martin kept blinking and looked flushed. She watched his trembling fingers reach inside his shirt and pull out a pack of cigarettes. Jack couldn't seem to get a cigarette out. His shaking fingers kept fumbling with the package. Finally the last cigarette emerged. Jack stuck it in his mouth and quickly flicked his small silver lighter. His first long puff seemed to quiet him some.

Suddenly Ann saw *it*. In English across the front of the empty pack was a large red target with the black lettering "Lucky Strike." Ann choked. Everything about that pack of cigarettes screamed they were Americans. If the German soldier saw it, he'd be all over Jack in an instant.

Jack casually wadded up the pack and tossed it toward the open window. The wad hit the windowsill and bounced back into the coach, landing beside the foot of the German soldier.

Ann tried not to cough or breathe. She looked at Jack with an intense stare that should have burned a hole in his head. For a moment Jack glanced back with a puzzled look in his eyes. Ann changed her focus and stared at the pack on the floor.

Jack blinked several times and then tilted forward, looking at the spot where Ann's eyes were fastened. His mouth dropped and he jerked back against the seat. A look of panic shot across his face.

Ann kept watching the German soldier. The man appeared oblivious to what was happening around him and had not turned back to her. But if the bouncing and winding of the tram caused the cigarette package to roll it could easily tumble out into the center of the car. The German wouldn't miss seeing the pack then. Her heart kept thumping like it might explode.

O Lord, please put a shelter of protection around us, Ann prayed. *You alone can keep that German from seeing the package that could betray all of us. Please, please keep Your hand on us right now.*

Jack closed his eyes. Ann couldn't tell whether he was praying or trying to deal with the pain. She'd bet on both.

The tram slowed and the photo shop appeared up ahead. They would have to get off at the next stop. She cleared her throat and both Americans looked at her. Ann stood up. They followed her lead. This time Hank would have to help Jack off the tram without her assistance. She started toward the door. The German winked again but Ann refused to encourage him.

When the tram pulled to a halt, Ann briskly walked down the stairs and stood on the sidewalk. To her surprise the German soldier kept trying to get her attention and didn't notice the two Americans walk by him. Reluctantly, she smiled back and kept his flirtation focused on her. The German stood like he was considering getting off. Immediately Ann turned and walked away, praying the Americans would get off the coach instantly. With her back turned, she waited until she heard the tram pull away. Turning slowly, she saw Jack and Hank standing by a light pole. Once again, Jack had a look of severe pain on his face, but the German had stayed on the tram.

Ann felt like her legs might fold up under her. Breathing deeply, she could still feel her heart pounding. With definite, steady steps she walked back to the two Americans. Jack's face was covered with a hangdog look.

"Your cigarettes could have cost us our lives," Ann snapped with barely restrained anger.

Jack nearly fell forward. "Oh heavens! I can't believe I made that mistake!" His face turned even more pale. "I'm so, so sorry. Madame Brusselman, forgive me. I apologize with everything I have."

Ann nodded. "Please, please don't ever do anything like that again." She turned and walked toward the photo shop. Ann Brusselman did not want to have an experience like this one anytime soon.

———

Not far from the center of Brussels on an obscure side street, Germany maintained an SS office that, by October 1943, everyone in the area knew was the Gestapo headquarters. Crammed next to the adjacent buildings, the three-story edifice looked like every other structure on the block. Nevertheless, the innocuous front of the red-brick building only concealed the diabolical activities of the Nazi war machine. In the back of the building, four men hovered around a wooden conference table, talking and awaiting Arnwolf Mandel's arrival. Colonel Bern Schmidt of the *Wehrmacht*'s Army Group B, Sixth army, sat across the table from Berg Heydrich, a distant relative of Reinhard Heydrich, the Gestapo chief. Consequently, Berg Heydrich always received special deference at such SS gatherings. Two assistants stood behind each of them.

The men stopped talking when they heard the sound of an automobile pulling up behind the building. Moments later the back door opened and Arnwolf Mandel walked in with Karl Herrick following him.

"*Seig Heil!*" Berg Heydrich snapped as he leaped to his feet.

"*Seig Heil!*" Mandel and Herrick instantly responded.

The three leaders sat down again with Karl Herrick standing behind Mandel. Berg Heydrich snapped his fingers, and immediately one of his assistants poured drinks for the men.

"Good to see you again," Colonel Bern Schmidt began, "I understand you will be working out of these offices in Brussels."

Arnwolf Mandel smiled. "*Ya!*" He nodded politely to Berg Heydrich. "I am looking forward to my time here with this group of professionals."

"As soon as we received the notification from Berlin of your coming," Berg said, "we prepared an office for you here in this building."

Mandel nodded a friendly thank-you.

"As you know, my relationship with the Gestapo is highly unusual," Colonel Schmidt said. "Our common objectives have created this unique opportunity for all of us to serve *Der Führer*."

"And what are those objectives?" Arnwolf asked with a decided coldness.

"The *Wehrmacht* remains concerned to capture all Allied soldiers on the run," Schmidt said. "We believe that a number of these escapees are still hiding in this area. The problem calls for us to work together."

"Like the two flyboys you let escape on the Sambre Meuse River?" Arnwolf sounded aloof and condescending.

Colonel Schmidt eyed him with a slight look of puzzlement. "Something of that order," he said slowly.

"I am committed to capturing every Allied dog that drops out of the sky and shooting them the instant they are found," Arnwolf's voice became more intense. "I intend to be relentless in my quest for these swine that are sworn enemies of the *Reich*."

Heydrich stared at Mandel as if surprised by the viciousness of his response. "We-l-l," Berg said with a long pause, "we are all committed to this task and appreciate your enthusiasm, Arnwolf. Yes, of course, we have the same commitment."

"And I am still in pursuit of those two men who evaded us that day we chased them down the Sambre Meuse River," Arnwolf said. "I am sure you are aware that I returned the next day and captured a British airman being concealed on the Groot Vogel farm. In the dangerous struggle to take this prisoner, I was forced to shoot him as well as the owner of the farm. I remain prepared to pursue these criminals on a night-and-day basis."

"No, I didn't know." Colonel Bern Schmidt pulled out a silver cigarette holder and took out a cigarette. He tapped it slowly on the back of the metal box. "You are certainly ready to roll for the chase, Arnwolf."

"*Absolutely.*" Arnwolf jutted his fat chin forward.

Schmidt glanced at Heydrich who sat carefully studying Mandel. "I suppose our questions about predisposition for readiness are answered, Berg. You have a new comrade who delights in the hunt. Let us simply agree to keep each other informed about what we find. When you have a man on the run, let us know and we will bring our forces to bear on the problem." Schmidt tapped his cigarette in an ash tray. "I will do the same."

"I requested Berlin to authorize me to work in the Brussels and Antwerp areas as I feel this is the route that these Allied prisoners are likely to take in trying to evade us. I presume that my work will be independent though cooperative." Arnwolf looked sternly at both Schmidt and Heydrich.

"Of course," Berg Heydrich said dryly.

"Good!" Arnwolf stood up and thrust his arm straight forward. "*Seig Heil!*"

The rest of the men in the room returned the salute.

"If you will excuse me. I will set up my offices and begin my work at once." Mandel marched out of the room with Herrick following him. The door slammed behind them.

"Interesting," Colonel Schmidt said. "You have added a new steamroller to your offices."

Berg Heydrich's eye's narrowed. "Steamroller? We shall see. I would prefer a roller to a blower." Heydrich pointed to the door and the rest of the men standing around the table quickly vanished, shutting it behind them.

Bern Schmidt glanced around the room to make sure no one was listening to their conversation. "Look, Berg. We've known each other for more than three decades. I joined the *Wehrmacht* and you signed on with the Gestapo because of your cousin Reinhard. If we weren't good friends, I would have never gotten into this, shall we say, 'relationship' with the SS." He leaned forward and spoke in a whisper. "What do you make of this Arnwolf Mandel character?"

Berg Heydrich swallowed the half-empty glass of cognac on the table. "He's straight out of the funny papers." Heydrich's eyes became cold and hard. "A cartoon character. Germany is full of nutcake crazies these days. The man is a fanatic trying to impress all of us with his zeal. The truth is that Mandel is a crackpot."

"Then why do you tolerate him around here?"

Berg pursed his lips and shrugged. "The people in Berlin thrive on sending these passionate bigots running all over the countryside because every now and then they catch somebody. I do what I'm told." He leaned forward to speak as low as possible. "Pay attention to me, Bern. This war isn't going our way right now. I am concerned that the German war machine could collapse. We need to push these caricatures like Mandel to the front. If the Allies make a major landing out there somewhere on the coast, we want people like Mandel running around screaming '*Seig Heil*' while we disappear. Am I making sense?"

The colonel leaned back in his chair and didn't say anything for several seconds. "I had no idea you had such feelings," he said thoughtfully. "No idea."

"And you'd better pay attention to the drift that the war is taking."

Colonel Schmidt pulled nervously at the collar on his uniform. "You are so, so very right." He stood up. "Thanks for the advice. Take care, my friend. And keep your eye on this Mandel before he does something crazy." The colonel hurried out the back door.

CHAPTER TWELVE

During the three weeks following the trip for photos, Jack Martin and Hank Holt found life at 127 Rue d'Ixelles to be far better than they could have hoped for if they had been running through the fields. Jack's legs started healing, but he still walked with an obvious limp and struggled. The damage would be inhibiting when he started the dash to the English Channel. He noticed the weather getting colder, and news of the war indicated the picnic was over for the Germans.

A story surfaced from the underground that the military at Stalingrad, Russia, had plotted to overthrow Hitler, but the *Putsch* never came off. Apparently the generals felt Hitler had overextended the *Wehrmacht* and the war was reaching a dangerous two-front confrontation that Germany could not maintain. Madame Brusselman believed that even the rumored existence of such a plan meant trouble was brewing inside the *Wehrmacht*. When the report reached the Brusselmans that the Allies had invaded the Italian peninsula and were forcing the Italians to surrender, the Brusselman household broke into ecstasy. Mussolini had been replaced by Marshal Pietro Badoglio who signed an armistice with the Allies.

At the same time, other reports increased that the Nazis had stepped up the liquidation of Jews. Two thousand Jews in Minsk, Belorussia, disappeared. Jews in the Sobibor death camp were executed as well as a thousand Jews in Przemysl, Poland. The reports were sobering.

While Julien toiled in his downstairs office that faced Rue d'Ixelles Street, Madame Brusselman worked upstairs training Jack and Hank to "act" French as well as learn basic procedures for the Comete Line escape route. She pushed the men to get themselves prepared and demanded that Jack force himself to walk around her apartment for hours. The endless strolls from room to room and back again remained difficult.

In the late afternoon, Jack walked out to the terrace that overlooked Rue d'Ixelles. Small pebbles in the gravel pressed into his feet and gave him spasmodic flashes of pain. For a few moments he looked down on the street below and then sat down in one of the chairs beside a little metal table. The fall wind picked up and gave him a cold jolting sensation. Across the street he could see the tile roofs of houses on the other side of the street. Smoke drifted leisurely into the low hanging clouds. Jack took a deep breath and let the breeze wash over his face.

The pain from the burns never stopped. Although his legs had definitely improved, the throbbing didn't cease. Taking old Grandpa Hennie Matthys's advice seriously, he intended to endure no matter what the cost. However, at moments like this when Jack was completely alone, he allowed the truth to well up in him. This afternoon was one of those times that he couldn't push reality aside.

Jack Martin didn't believe he could survive the dash out of the country.

He lit up a cigarette and let the smoke curl up toward the sky. If the Nazis caught him, they'd probably kill him on the spot. He feared putting Hank Holt in a bind where his friend might be slowed down and captured. Jack had already strained Ann Brusselman's friendship to the max with the incident of the empty pack of cigarettes bouncing around on the floor of the tram. The truth was that everybody would be better off if he simply disappeared into the city of Brussels and left them free to do what had to be done. Of course, Jack's limitations made it impossible for him to get very far by himself. A man on crutches always remained easily identifiable. His condition had to be a bad omen for the future.

Of course, life on the Texas prairie had been difficult during the Great Depression, but he didn't remember the past that way. Sure, the Martin family was poor, but everybody was poor. Not having much didn't make much difference when nobody else had anything either. Struggling to keep the farm running while the drought devastated the countryside had certainly been a struggle. For a little boy like young Jack, there wasn't any physical pain, and that was the difference in where he was today. Suffering turned the thumbscrews on Jack.

A rattlesnake had once crawled across the wooden planks of their Texas back porch and curled up in a dark corner. Jack had just gone out the back door when he heard that terrifying buzzing sound beside him. The snake's black eyes stared at Jack like he was the target in a Texas shoot-out. The sound of the tail and the coiled snake ready to strike made his blood turn cold. With one giant leap, Jack had bounded off the back porch, screaming at the top of his lungs.

"Maw! Please! Come out and save me. There's a rattler on the back porch!"

His mother had called for Jack's father to come home and kill the snake. Jack stood in the dry grass and stared at the coiled snake that wouldn't stop clattering with that awful tail sticking straight up in the air. Jack knew he was going to die. He kept screaming like a wild man.

Eventually Jack's father came around the side of the house carrying an old axe handle. "Stand back, son. I'll take care of that critter for you."

Jack's old man had beaten the ugly creature to death and thereafter always insisted the battle was "no big deal." As far as Jack had been concerned, it *was* a big deal. For an hour Jack had sat on the back porch and stared at the dead snake. Those blank eyes never quit terrifying him.

The truth was that his situation at 127 Rue d'Ixelles had proved to be another Great Depression going on inside his head, with Nazi vipers lurking on all the street corners with the same deadly stare. He guessed there was no alternative but to keep on trying like his family had done for an entire decade in Texas. His problem was basic. Jack remained certain he would die before he escaped.

————

Two days had passed since Jack Martin sat out on the terrace and thought about his struggle. The weather kept getting cooler and November meant the snow would soon be falling. No one ever called in the morning.

At 10:00 a.m., the telephone rang.

Jack and Hank froze in their chairs and waited for Ann Brusselman to do something, *anything*. The phone rang again.

"Hello," Ann said softly.

For a few a moments she stood listening intently and then hung up the phone. "That was Julien downstairs. He's received word the Gestapo is going to raid this building in a matter of minutes."

Jack lunged forward in his chair and grabbed Hank's arm.

"No!" Ann said sternly. "Don't move. Julien said you will not have time to escape. You must get on your working clothes and pretend to be cleaning my walls. He doesn't know why they are coming here." Ann ran her hands nervously through her hair. "Maybe someone has betrayed us." She began pacing back and forth, wringing her hands. "I don't know. I just don't know." Ann stopped. "Get those photo IDs and put your work clothes on!"

Hank shot into the bedroom. Jack pushed himself up out of the chair and hobbled across the room at a far slower pace while Ann ran to the telephone to call the Somervilles, the other family in the building who worked with the underground. As soon as the call was made, Ann rushed to the terrace to watch the street. She stopped abruptly and ran back inside.

"Remember!" Ann shouted. "Jack will speak German if questions are asked and I will talk for Hank since he speaks only English. We can only pray they don't push Hank for answers."

"We'll keep our ID cards handy," Jack said through the door.

"And I'll get buckets with water for washing walls," Hank added. "We'll get in position as soon as we can change clothes."

"Hurry!" Ann demanded and ran back to the terrace.

Up the street Ann could see men blocking the entire Rue d'Ixelles boulevard off. They had stopped the tram and were not letting citizens through. Turning in the opposite direction, Ann saw German soldiers doing the same thing on the other end of the long street. As she watched, city police and army vehicles began emerging and driving toward their building. From out of the conglomeration of officers, Ann identified men in long black leather coats wearing regular street hats directing the parade of traffic. They had to be Gestapo agents. The cars and trucks formed a semicircle in front of their apartment building and stopped.

"Get in place!" the fat man wearing a black fedora shouted

to the soldiers. "We must be ready for resistance. Shoot if necessary!"

"God, help us," Ann prayed aloud. "Please keep us from being betrayed. Oh Lord! Protect us."

The sounds of buckets sloshing water echoed out of the dinning room. Ann turned and watched the two Americans dipping rags into the water and wringing them out. At least, everyone was ready. The Gestapo would be banging on their door in a matter of seconds.

"Follow me!" The heavyset Gestapo agent's voice floated upward as he pointed at the front door and then waved for soldiers to break in. "Break in!" After the first row of soldiers hit the building, the fat man followed them inside the building.

Ann looked over the edge. Apparently, they had not entered Julien's office, but seemed to have gone into some other part of the building. Ann caught her breath. The only other unit in the building they could be interested in was the Somerville family.

She listened intently, trying to hear the sound of men rushing up the stairs. Nothing happened. No noise came through the door. Once more Ann looked over the rail to see what was happening on the street. After several minutes, the Germans started coming out. The heavyset Gestapo officer marched out with a blonde-haired young man in tow. The youth had his hands behind his back with metal handcuffs locked in place. With complete indifference, the officer slammed the youth up against the side of a car. In that moment Ann saw the young man's face.

The lad was Dirk Vogel!

Another agent in a black leather coat came hustling out of the building with a woman also in handcuffs.

"Get in there!" the Gestapo agent shouted at the boy.

Without a word, Dirk slid in the backseat of the car. The second agent pushed the woman in the other side.

"Maria Somerville!" Ann gasped. "They've caught her!"

"Found him lurking in a back closet," the agent told one of the policemen in such a loud voice he could be heard from the balcony. "We've been following this kid for days. Go ahead and question the rest of the people downstairs. I don't expect you'll find anything else. We'll take them back to our offices."

The policeman saluted and the car drove off.

Madame Brusselman stared in astonishment. Their apartment had gone untouched.

CHAPTER THIRTEEN

During the trek to the SS headquarters in Brussels, Arnwolf Mandel kept turning in the seat and staring menacingly at Dirk Vogel. Maria Somerville sat next to Dirk with a stern, aloof look on her face. After several blocks, Mandel spoke.

"We've been following you for some time, Vogel," Mandel said. "There's no point in maintaining silence." He shook his finger in Vogel's face. "We followed you directly to the Somerville apartment. You led us there," Mandel chuckled.

Vogel said nothing.

"You're young. You have plenty of life ahead. Your mother needs you. Right?"

Dirk stared at the floorboard.

Arnwolf Mandel turned around to Karl Herrick, the driver. "Take the alley route. We'll go in the back door."

Herrick nodded. "Certainly."

"Our agents are most persistent," Mandel turned back to Dirk. "If you talk honestly and openly with us, you will save yourself considerable time as well as pain."

Dirk didn't answer.

"The same is true for you, Madame Somerville," Mandel barked at the woman. "I don't like hurting a woman, but we will oblige if necessary."

Maria Somerville's lips trembled, but she didn't speak.

"Whatever," Mandel shrugged. "We can force you both to speak, you know."

Karl Herrick turned the roadster to the left and down the alley behind the building that housed the Gestapo. Pulling up behind the back door, he stopped. The two men hustled Dirk Vogel and Madame Somerville inside and into the conference room where Mandel had first met Berg Heydrich and talked with Colonel Schmidt again. Karl Herrick pushed Dirk Vogel into a wooden chair. Herrick quickly tied him to the chair back and set another chair in front of Vogel. As soon as he had Dirk Vogel secured, he pushed Maria Somerville into an adjacent room.

"Okay," Mandel began, sitting in the chair across from Vogel. "You can start by telling us about this so-called Comete Line underground system." He slipped leather gloves on.

Dirk jumped when Arnwolf Mandel said "Comete Line."

"Didn't think we knew about the organization, did you?" Mandel sneered. "You must recognize that the Third Reich has supreme knowledge. We give resistance people plenty of rope to allow them to hang themselves."

Dirk blinked several times but maintained his silence.

"Nothing to say?" Arnwolf Mandel shrugged. He swirled and hit Dirk squarely in the mouth. Mandel's leather gloves popped against his lips and sent Dirk's head flying backward. Dirk's lower lip split and blood ran down his chin.

"There are many ways to communicate," Mandel continued. "Let me try another route." The SS agent hit the young man in the stomach with a fierce uppercut. Vogel gasped in pain.

Karl Herrick walked back into the room.

"You country boys don't seem to understand that we are in a war." Mandel kept pounding his fists against his thick leather gloves. "We're not part of some nice, pleasant afternoon tea party, you understand." The SS agent hit Dirk in the side of his face with everything he had. The chair tipped sideways, falling to the floor and bouncing Dirk's head on the wood.

Vogel's eyes stayed shut. The young man's face became even whiter.

"Pick him up!" Mandel snarled at Herrick. "Set him upright and hold the chair this time."

Herrick labored to pick up the chair with Vogel tied securely to the back. Vogel groaned and slowly opened his glazed eyes.

"I'm trying to be your friend," Arnwolf whispered. "You're making it difficult." Once again he punched Vogel squarely in the nose with a violent right thrust, causing blood to gush from Dirk's nose. "You're hard to help." Arnwolf winked at Karl Herrick. "I guess I'll have to be more specific."

Arnwolf lit into a flurry of blows, punching Dirk in the body and across the face. He kept up the pounding until the over-weight Mandel stopped to catch his breath.

"He's unconscious," Karl Herrick said. "I don't think he could talk if he wanted to."

"Okay," Mandel puffed. "Let's go work on the woman for a while."

Jack Martin hobbled to the terrace to watch the street below him while the Gestapo's arrests created a significant upheaval up and down the boulevard. Madame Brusselman did not call her husband waiting downstairs because her telephone line might have been tapped. For a long time Hank, Ann, and Jack watched the street to see if the Gestapo would return. Eventually, the police removed the barricades and allowed the tram to run through. When the traffic resumed, Jack said nothing and life on Rue d'Ixelles returned to normal. Thirty minutes later the front door opened and Julien rushed in.

"My dear!" Julien exclaimed. "Are you all right?"

Ann ran to her husband as soon as he stepped over the threshold and hugged him fiercely. "I thought for sure they were coming to arrest us."

"I understand." Julien held Ann. "I got a call from Reverend Harold Assink just before they blocked off the streets. His people had discovered that Gestapo agents were following Dirk Vogel. That was the tip-off because I knew Dirk wouldn't come to our house without calling first. I was sure the Americans were safe."

"Oh, Julien!" Ann hugged her husband again. "I was terrified they would grab us, but when I saw Dirk led out in handcuffs I felt even worse. The poor boy!" Ann started crying.

Julien led her to the couch where they huddled together. The two American pilots sat down across from them. For several minutes no one spoke. Finally Julien began again.

"I am sure they will eventually make Dirk talk." Julien shook his head. "He will be ruthlessly tortured and eventually something will come out. Possibly Dirk will mention us. I simply don't know." Julien shrugged. "Our apartment will no longer be viable. We must not jeopardize the Comete Line operation."

Jack shook his head. "We understand and are ready to leave this minute if necessary. You have been more than friends to us."

"No, no. I will have to make the arrangements first, but I must assume that we will need to move you today," Julien said. "Are you prepared?"

"We have nothing," Jack said. "We can be ready to leave in minutes."

"I am sorry," Ann said. "We would never have planned such a hasty exit."

"Ma'am," Hank said. "You've treated us like royalty. We'll always owe you an eternal debt. No problem for us to get on the road."

"No problem *except me*," Jack added. "My legs don't work well and I'm sure that I'll need crutches. If that's a problem I can—"

"None whatsoever," Julien cut him off. "We will factor in that need as we make our arrangements."

"Stop," Jack protested, "I'm not sure what I'll do, but if it is necessary I'll—"

"No problem," Julien again countered him. "Don't worry. I'll let our contacts know about this need." He studied Jack for a minute. "Can you ... can you walk any significant distance without the crutches?"

"I walk around here because my steps are slow and the furniture protects me. I imagine I could walk a short distance through a terminal at a slow pace without crutches. Beyond that ... I just don't know."

"I understand." Julien nodded his head. "Let me see what I can arrange."

Julien Brusselman walked quickly to his telephone. For a few minutes he talked to someone on the other end of the line. Ann hurried around the house nervously adjusting knick-knacks and pieces of furniture.

For the first time, Jack Martin realized Julien was the unseen pillar of support that held the family together. Ann's strength and assurance had always been supported by this foundation, keeping the family intact. While Yvonne and Jacques were usually around the house only in the late afternoon and evenings, they leaned on their father as well for the courage to keep up their struggle. When he walked back into the living room, Julien's easygoing features had changed into a firm, fixed countenance of authority.

"We will not have much time," Julien said sternly. "You two men must be on the 6:00 train leaving tonight. The connections will be close."

"This is an emergency switch of plans?" Ann asked.

Julien nodded. "No one was prepared for the surprise attack today. Our options have been reduced, but headquarters believes it is paramount that Jack and Hank get out of Brussels immediately."

"What's happened?" Ann pressed.

"Of course, the underground did not know that for some time Dirk Vogel was being followed. His capture exposed us in areas that we hadn't anticipated." Julien stared out the window. "No one is sure where Dirk had come from or was going today. You see, that's our problem. He may have exposed more of our contacts to the Gestapo than Dirk had any idea existed out there. Our people think that our only hope is to get our house back to normal immediately. That means getting Jack and Hank on the road at once."

Ann took a deep breath. "I see," she said slowly and then dried her eyes. "I must get myself ready." She straightened and the look of fear vanished from her face. "We must make ready."

"The underground believes it is better for you to take the Americans to the train station than me," Julien added. "My position in the gas company downstairs makes me a prime target. Further, these men must go down the back stairs at intervals. They don't want anyone to see them together until you reach the train station. Then there will be so many people, it won't make any difference. Headquarters wants you to take Yvonne and Jacques with you."

Ann nodded. "I am prepared. Who will meet us at the train station?"

"They can't tell me," Julien explained. "You will need to walk in and someone who knows you will show up." He wrung his hands. "I know that's not much to go on and puts you in a bad position, but that's all they could tell me right now."

"I see," Ann's voice trembled. "I guess we have no choice."

"My crutches?" Jack asked.

"We-l-l," Julien said slowly. "I think we will wrap them in newspaper before you leave this house and then you will carry them through the terminal. At least concealment will provide some cover."

"Okay." Jack shook his legs. "I'll start getting limbered up. Unfortunately, I will need to walk slowly."

"We'll adjust," Ann said. "Let's start getting ready." She walked into the kitchen.

Jack followed Ann and cornered her in the kitchen. He began slowly. "I don't understand. The pieces in this puzzle don't fit together. I want to know why you'd put yourself at such risk. Your husband? Your children? Everything you own at stake for a couple of Americans from out of nowhere? Why?"

For a moment Ann looked out the window. "Jesus once said, 'a new commandment I give to you, that you love one another; even as I have loved you, that you also love one another.' He spoke of a love that can exceed the limitations of the human heart. What we do is our feeble attempt to express such a love to demonstrate His love."

Jack stared. He didn't know what to do or say. Finally he turned around and walked back into the living room.

"Time is running out," Julien warned. "We must hurry." He disappeared into the bedroom.

Jack stood by his chair and watched everyone moving rapidly about the house. The Brusselmans and Hank hurried about their work, but for a moment Jack wanted to drink in every detail of the room and remember this apartment exactly for how it was during the time they had lived there. He could never forget how important these four walls had been for them. The truth was that the Brusselmans at 127 Rue d'Ixelles had demonstrated love and saved their lives.

Jack Martin watched cars fly past while the Brusselmans' vehicle wound slowly toward the train station. For the moment, life seemed normal in Brussels, but Jack kept worrying that Julien Brusselman might have a visit from the Gestapo that night. Since the rest of the family were in the car with him, they were safe for the moment.

Madame Brusselman pulled her car up to the curb in front of the train terminal. "Get out carefully," she told Jack. "I am going to have my son Jacques stand with you. You'll look like ordinary citizens." She glanced up and down the street. "We will come back as quickly as possible."

Jack nodded and slid out of the car. Little Jacques got out of the backseat and took his hand. The Brusselmans' car roared away. Jack and Jacques walked slowly toward the lamppost.

Jack smiled at his little friend. Jacques grinned back and didn't say anything but Jack caught a look of fear in the little boy's eyes. Standing on the curb in the middle of a German-controlled city wasn't the safest place in the world to wait.

Fifty feet away Jack saw two German soldiers walking toward him with a police dog on a leash. Large, strong-looking men, the Germans seemed more like farm boys out for a stroll. No one spoke, and people walking close to the troops got out of their way. The soldiers kept inching toward him.

Jack turned and walked stiffly toward the entrance of the terminal. Jacques followed him, clutching his hand tightly. When he reached the door, Jack leaned against the wall and watched the Germans only ten feet away. He could feel his heart pounding hard. After a few moments, Jack looked back. The soldiers had walked on by.

Jack's entire body sagged. He took a deep breath and shot a glance at Jacques. The little boy stood resolutely beside him, staring at the sidewalk like he'd never look up again.

"We're okay," Jack said in English.

Jacques looked up and nodded. "*Oui.*"

Five minutes later Ann Brusselman came walking up with

her arm in Hank Holt's like they were a family. Yvonne carried Jack's newspaper-wrapped crutches.

"Ready to go." Ann smiled a deceptively carefree smile. "Let's walk in. I'm sure the right people will find us."

Jack nodded. "Let's do it." He turned stiffly toward the entrance.

The two Americans and the three Belgians sauntered casually into the busy terminal where people were rushing back and forth, hurrying to catch their trains. High up in the center of the front wall on a large signboard, whirling, constantly changing signs indicated where the trains were going. All around the open area, German soldiers stood watching the passengers.

"Don't panic," Ann said softly. "The station is always this chaotic. Just walk slowly toward the signboard. Someone will show up."

Jack continued his stiff-legged, steady gait. Jacques clutched his hand even more tightly.

Suddenly a tall, thin man with dark brown hair walked straight toward the five friends. Wearing a heavy overcoat and a brown felt hat, he gave a casual wave. "Why, Ann! Good to see you!"

"Reverend Harold Assink!" Ann looked startled. "How nice to run into you here at the train terminal."

"Yes, yes." Assink hugged Ann and whispered something in her ear. "I heard you were leaving town with your children and wanted to wish you well."

Ann's mouth dropped. "With my children?"

"How nice that you could make this unexpected visit to Paris. It so happens that I will be on the same train with you. Isn't this wonderful?"

Ann blinked several times. "Yes. Of course. Yes. Certainly."

"We will have time to talk about many things." Reverend Assink kept smiling. "Yes. We can explain many things since we will all be sitting together."

"Sitting together?" Ann kept nodding but her eyes looked mystified.

Assink shoved a small envelope into her hand. "A little greeting card from my wife. You will want to read it *immediately* before you try to board." He suddenly looked at her sternly. "*Before*," he repeated.

"Yes. Yes, of course." Ann forced a smile.

"Why don't you read the card and then you can board the train," Reverend Assink said. "I'll meet you after you are seated." He nodded politely and hurried away.

Ann swallowed hard and watched the minister disappear into the crowd. With trembling hands, she opened the small card. Inside she found five tickets for the train ride to Paris with a significant amount of French francs.

"I guess we're all going," Jack said. "You okay with that arrangement?"

"No," Ann kept the forced smile in place. "No, not at all. Something's gone wrong." She swallowed hard. "Let's get on that train and get out of here."

CHAPTER FOURTEEN

The Brussels city terminal accommodated trains coming and going on sundry tracks that halted behind the entry gates. Far overhead open glass ventilators on the roof allowed smoke and steam to escape into the sky. Madame Brusselman paused to read the note before herding her charges through the turnstile and down the sidewalk toward train 105. She dropped the card in the trash. Just as they reached the coach, four men in civilian clothes appeared out of nowhere, blocking the entrance to the car.

"Checking papers," the short, squatty man said with a German accent. "Present identification." The other men stood by him with their arms crossed over their chests, gawking menacingly.

Ann forced a smile and pulled out the papers for her and the children. The agent looked carefully and gestured for her to move on.

Hank Holt handed his photo ID without saying a word. Once more the agent studied the form and his face before gesturing for Hank to walk on past.

Jack Martin took a deep breath and stepped forward as casually as possible.

"Papers!" the agent snapped.

"*Ya,*" Jack answered in German.

The agent looked at him curiously. "*Bestimmung?*"

"Paris." Jack held out the ticket.

"Humph!" the agent nodded and looked hard at his face. "*Weitergehen.*"

Jack smiled and forced himself to walk forward as naturally as possible but he couldn't help hobbling. When he reached for the handrail to board, Jack looked back. The agent kept watching him. With a supreme effort, he forced himself up the step. He could feel the tender skin on his shins cracking. For a moment the pain felt like an electric shock but he kept moving up the steps into the coach.

The rest of the party stood at the top, watching him with fear in their eyes. As soon as he reached the last step, the Brusselman children led the way to their seats. The car was only partially filled, giving them ample space.

Jack dropped on the seat and grabbed his knees. "I'm bleeding," he whispered to Hank. "But I don't think it's going to be a big problem."

"What do you want me to do?" Hank said.

"Just keep an eye on my pants to make sure the blood stops before I leave an identifiable stain."

Hank nodded and looked out the window apprehensively to see if the agents were still watching. They were.

"What do you think happened?" Jack groaned.

Ann shook her head. "Don't know. Just don't know. Harold Assink whispered in my ear that we shouldn't worry." After a few seconds, Ann said, "Those men were Gestapo watching who boarded the train. You got by but they studied your faces far too carefully."

Jack closed his eyes for a minute. "That was cutting it close."

"Too close," Hank said.

"I have my instructions," Ann said. "We will go all the way to Paris. For the moment you can relax."

For several minutes no one spoke. A few more people boarded the train. The sound of the conductor yelling for everyone to board immediately echoed from the outside. Reverend Harold Assink entered from the back and sat down a few seats behind them. He looked out the window as if he didn't know anyone in the coach.

The train started to pull out. Harold Assink never looked away from the window. The car began to pick up more momentum heading south toward France. In a few minutes the suburbs of Brussels disappeared and the train picked up full speed. Assink didn't move until a full ten minutes after they left the station. Only then did he get up and walk toward Madame Brusselman and her travelers.

"I think we are safe now," Assink said. "If the SS knew who you were, the Gestapo would have arrested you on the spot before you got on the train. Of course, they gave you the third degree check."

"Why are we here?" Ann blurted out. "I didn't expect that I and the children would be on the train."

"We don't know what's going on," Reverend Assink said. "Moreover, we don't know if Madame Somerville or Dirk Vogel will talk and how much they might say. For the safety of you and the children, headquarters thought we should get you out of town for at least several days until we have more insight."

"You will know for sure?" Ann pressed.

Assink nodded. "I can't talk about it, but eventually we will. Your leaving the city gives us additional time to assess every detail."

"And Julien?"

Reverend Assink patted Ann's hand. "Julien will go on working at the gas company. One of our people will come by to see him this evening and give him all of this information. Don't fret, he will be fine."

"Don't fret?" Jack forced a cynical smile. "How can anyone not worry, friend. We are all under the eye of death."

"Oh, no!" Assink's eyes flashed. "We are under *the eye of God* and that makes all the difference in the world!"

"I hope so," Jack said.

"Don't hope!" Assink suddenly sounded like a preacher. "No! *Believe!*" He shook his finger as if making a point in a sermon. Realizing that he looked like an orator, Reverend Assink quickly folded his fingers and tried to appear casual.

Jack watched Yvonne and Jacques sitting snugly against their mother. Both children looked worried. Such a trip into the dark night had to etch painful memories in their minds. He closed his eyes and leaned against the seat. The experience was sure carving unforgettable recollections in his head.

———————

Night had fallen over Brussels by the time Karl Herrick dragged Dirk Vogel back into the interrogation room and flopped him down in the same chair Arnwolf Mandel used when the SS agent started beating the young man. Dirk's face remained swollen with one eye completely shut and his lips broken. He looked more dazed than coherent. Herrick tied him firmly in the chair.

"Has the woman confessed anything?" Mandel demanded.

Herrick shook his head. "Tough as a boot. She's lying on the floor unconscious but I got nothing out of her. I have two other men in there who'll start working on her as soon as she comes around."

Arnwolf Mandel rubbed his chin. "Surprising. We'll keep rubbing salt on her wounds. You ready to start on Vogel again?"

Herrick nodded. "The metal tub is on the table with the mallet."

"Let's start." Mandel pointed to the bell-shaped hunk of metal. "Help me get this over Vogel's head."

The two men picked up the heavy tub and placed it over Dirk's head, resting it on his shoulders. Mandel picked up the mallet. "Let's see if our boy likes the little tune I'm going to play."

Mandel hit the side of the tub-shaped bell as hard as he could. A deep resonant ringing filled the room, making the sound inside the tub deafening. Before the roaring had died out, Mandel hit the bell again. He kept beating on the metal ceaselessly for fifteen minutes. Finally he laid the mallet on the table.

"Let's take it off Vogel," Mandel told Herrick. "Put this heavy thing back on the floor."

The two men lifted the tub off Dirk Vogel. Vogel's eyes had a wild look and he couldn't seem to hear Arnwolf Mandel speaking.

"Drag him over here to the 'German Chair,'" Mandel said. "I think a little pressure on his spine will help loosen his tongue."

Herrick untied Vogel and dragged him to the strange chair sitting at the side of the room. As the back headrest was lowered, an inner lever put unbearable pressure in the middle of the person's back. The "German Chair" could eventually crush the victim's spine. Herrick quickly buckled Vogel into the chair.

"Can you hear me?" Mandel shouted in Dirk's face.

Dirk opened his good eye. For a moment he looked at Mandel incoherently.

"Hear me?" Mandel screamed again.

Slowly Dirk shook his head.

"I want to know what you did with those two pilots that you helped escape," Mandel demanded. "Tell me about them."

Dirk said nothing.

"Put the pressure on him!"

Herrick started lowering the headrest. Vogel screamed.

"Now let me start again." Mandel pulled a chair in front of Vogel. "We can crush the life out of you or you can give me a few simple answers. Tell me about the two men."

Dirk blinked a couple of times. "I don't know where they are."

"More pressure."

Herrick twisted the headrest farther down and Vogel screamed.

"Tell me!" Mandel shouted.

"One man ... had burns ... limped," Vogel gasped. "Don't know ... where ... are."

"Hit him again."

Herrick pushed farther. Vogel gasped and slumped forward.

"I'll kill him if I push much more," Herrick said.

"A man with a limp!" Mandel smiled. "We're making some progress. Two men running and one has bad burns."

The door opened and an SS agent entered. "We've tortured the woman nearly to death. She won't tell us about any other underground contacts. I don't think she'll live much longer."

Arnwolf Mandel got up from the chair slowly. "We haven't gotten much out of them." He started pacing. "We do know they are with the underground. I've learned a little from this

Dutch fool. Go back and work on the French woman some more. We'll keep it up for another thirty minutes."

"Whatever you say." The SS agent left the room.

The long gray coaches slowed and started pulling into the suburbs of Paris. Train 105 was on time. Jack Martin peered into the darkness. It was nearly midnight, and all lighting along the tracks had been turned off to prevent night bombing raids. All he could see was the vague shapes of buildings spinning past. Yvonne and Jacques sat fast asleep snuggled against their mother, whose eyes were closed. Hank Holt had also drifted off. Only Reverend Harold Assink remained awake.

"We will be in the center of the city shortly," Assink suddenly said. "A young woman named Monique Sernin will meet you. Monique speaks excellent English. She will lead you and Hank out of the station."

"I see," Jack said slowly. "What about Madame Brusselman and the children?"

"I will get off the train first. If there are no problems, I will come back for the Brusselman family and we will disappear into the station. You will not see us again."

"What will you do?"

Assink smiled. "We have many possibilities. Of course, our options are secret and you don't want to know in case you are captured. When all is secure, we will return to Brussels and our work will continue."

Everything sounded so simple, so straightforward. It wasn't. The entire process was treacherous with deadly consequences. All that needed to happen was for someone to make a false move, a wrong step, and the wrath of the Nazis would fall on all of them. Harold Assink sat there describing the details with a calm voice when his stomach had to be churning.

"Where will this Monique Sernin take us?" Jack asked.

"Monique will have a car. Even I do not know her destination, so I can't tell you. I do know this. You can and must trust her with your life. Do exactly what she says."

Jack nodded.

Silence fell between the two men while the train continued to slow down. Jack studied the minister. His thin face had a typical Dutch look but Assink's deep-set eyes were different. He kept looking about the coach, out the windows, at the people sleeping in their seats, assessing every aspect of the approach. Assink's eyes missed nothing. The man had a stability that amazed Jack.

"How do you do it?" Jack asked. "Anyone else would be scared to death."

"I believe in divine providence," Harold said soberly. "God is in control, not me. I thank Him that He is going to guide us through this approaching minefield."

"How do you know that's true?"

Assink shrugged. "Our people lived through a terrible time during the Protestant Reformation. Many were killed and a grueling war raged across our country. We learned to listen carefully to what the Scripture said. Do you know what the Bible says?"

"I am a Christian. Obviously there is much in the Bible that I don't know."

"In verse fifteen of the thirty-first Psalm, the book says, 'my times are in thy hands; deliver me from the hand of my enemies and persecutors!' Every day I quote this verse when I begin my work."

"My times are in thy hands," Jack repeated. "I will try to remember," Jack said. "My times are in His hands."

"That is our secret," Assink whispered. "We believe and trust that our God will lead us through the web that the spider of evil has spun."

Jack thought about Assink's answer for a moment. He didn't know if another pointed question was appropriate but he had to ask anyway. He leaned forward. "And why are you so willing to risk your lives for people you don't know? People like Hank and myself?"

The minister reached over and patted Jack on the hand. "We are all sailing on a great river. During these brief moments, God has put us in the same boat. We help each other because we are comrades in this important journey. Jesus taught us that we will be blessed when men revile and persecute us falsely on His account. Regardless of what happens to any of us, we can rejoice because we have a great reward in heaven."

The train slowed. Reverend Assink immediately began looking out the window, watching everything. "Wake up, my dear." He shook Ann Brusselman. "We are here." She stretched and looked out the window.

In a few minutes, the Brusselmans and Harold Assink would be gone forever. Jack must remember what he had heard. *All* their times were indeed in the hands of God.

PART THREE

The Run to the Ocean

CHAPTER FIFTEEN

*T*exas took on the expectant look in the spring. A smell of early rain hung in the air: tree-filled flatlands around Dallas stood particularly poised for a new season, branches were already tipped with green buds about to explode with new leaves. A few blades of new grass had pushed through the dead yellowish stubble left after months of a cold winter. Tulips and daffodils had forged ahead of the other flowers and their green blades stood three to four inches above the ground, while the flowers remained folded in the shafts ready to burst forth with vibrant color. In a couple of weeks Easter would arrive and then the changes would unfold.

The turning of the seasons always brought in the latest vogue. The spring fashions for 1957 appeared to be on the slightly formal side with ladies' hats leading the parade of style. White gloves added a touch of elegance, and girls wore cancan petticoats, flaring their dresses out in a wide circle. Young boys would buy a new tie to wear before Easter morning dawned. On this Sunday, two weeks before the special day, everything appeared to be in place.

Jack Martin looked around the church that he and Martha had attended for the past ten years since he had come back from the war and they had married. The smallness of the sanctuary fit Jack's taste and he liked the preacher. Little George and Mary Martin sat quietly on either side of him. Jack sat between the children because they'd fight with each other if he didn't. Of course, both of the kids knew that starting a ruckus would get them hauled out of the sanctuary in an instant.

Far off in the sky the roar of jet engines echoed through the small white building and interrupted Jack's thoughts. The whirling sound of a turbo-prop like the B-17 he had flown in the war had bothered him some, but the new sound was far more unsettling. The noise of *any* airplane startled him. He clutched his fingers together tightly.

The choir finished singing an anthem arranged around the old familiar hymn "Trust and Obey." Closing the music, they sat down with their usual flair. The pastor walked to the pulpit and started reading the lesson from the eleventh chapter of John's Gospel. Jack had heard most of the stories a thousand times and his mind tended to wander a bit.

"Now when Jesus came, he found that Lazarus had already been in the tomb four days," the pastor read. "Bethany was near Jerusalem, about two miles off . . ."

The words snapped Jack to attention. During the twelve years he had been home after the war Jack had done everything possible to force himself not to think about death. Even the mention of a grave froze him in place. He had never talked about the war with Martha and certainly not with the children. The idea of anyone locked in a tomb sent chills down his spine, and talk of someone dying made him extremely nervous.

"Lord, if you had been here, my brother would not have died," the minister kept reading.

With considerable persistence, Jack had tried not to think about Dirk Vogel or Madame Somerville. He pushed their faces from his mind, but hearing about a fatality made their countenances arise out of his memory and dance before his eyes. Their return from the abode of the dead left him feeling guilty and defensive for still being alive. Even sitting in a church, Jack felt disconcerted by the story of Lazarus.

For years after returning from Europe, Jack would wake up in the middle of the night screaming. Dreams of being chased by wolves interrupted his sleep and left him rolling in anguish across a landscape covered by sheets. Along the way he'd heard of post-traumatic stress disorder, but Jack Martin wasn't about to see a shrink and pour out his problems. He'd suck it up and go on. Such was the way of a Texas farm boy. None of this sissy breakdown stuff that filled the magazines.

After he finished one of those clandestine pep talks with himself, Jack knew he was wrong and needed help. Oh yes, he had a real problem, but Jack still couldn't bring himself to get medical attention.

"I know that he will rise again in the resurrection at the last day," the preacher said.

Dirk Vogel's face appeared before Jack's eyes. Tousled blond hair hanging down over a long narrow forehead. Long arms and legs of a typical Dutch boy. A sly grin on his young face. All the innocence and anticipation of a young man about to enter the big world suddenly cut short by the Gestapo. Jack felt tears edging into his eyes and he tried to fight them back.

Jack hated these moments when his emotions got out of control. People noticed. If they didn't, he sure did. Tears started trickling down his cheek. In his back pocket was a handkerchief, but he didn't want to look so obvious. The tears kept coming.

"Here, dear," Martha whispered and pressed a handkerchief in his palm. She kept looking straight ahead.

He guessed she'd gotten used to his problem and knew not to mention it. The children kept looking resolutely straight ahead with their eyes too fixed toward the front of the sanctuary not to have noticed he was crying. Jack dabbed at his eyes and tried to keep his face fixed.

"I am the resurrection and the life," the preacher read. "He who believes in me, though he die, yet shall he live, and whoever lives and believes in me shall never die."

Dirk Vogel had believed that promise. Probably Madame Somerville had too. Had the others? Had the men in his bombing crew?

Jack didn't know. But this promise had grown in his own life with each passing year. He clutched at the preacher's words as if he were Lazarus shrouded in the darkness, longing for someone to unbind him and set him free from the clutches of death. The words, the possibility, the hope rang through Jack's mind like a mallet striking a bell. He desperately needed to believe this story. Death wasn't some abstract idea being bantered back and forth between two college kids playing verbal ping-pong. Jack had stood toe-to-toe with the Black Specter standing with a scythe in hand ready to cut him down. He could still see those grim eyes peering into his own soul. If Jack needed anything, it was to believe in the promise that whoever lives and believes in Jesus will never die.

The minister closed the Bible and laid it on the pulpit. For a moment he looked across the congregation as if assessing the spiritual state of each one of them. "We need these words today," he concluded.

Jack's mind drifted back to yesterday . . .

Reverend Harold Assink hurried back into train 105. Midnight had covered Paris with blackness except for the few overhead lights that had been dimmed to protect the train station from bombing. By this time the coach had emptied of everyone except the Brusselmans and the two Americans. A feeling of emptiness hung in the air.

Assink trotted down the aisle. "No problems out there yet. Sure, German soldiers are floating around. At this hour of the night I don't think we should worry." He pointed toward the exit. "Monique Sernin will be waiting by the turnstile. She'll

take you into Paris. You can start using your crutches now."
Reverend Assink thrust his hand forward. "Good luck, gentlemen." He turned and hurried off the train.

Jack looked into the eyes of Ann Brusselman. "How can
we possibly thank you?" he said with profound sincerity. "You,
Julien, and the children have literally saved our lives."

"*Merci beaucoup* is how we say it," Ann said. She hugged
both men. "God bless you, Jack and Hank." She took Yvonne
and Jacques's hands, smiled, turned and hurried out of the
train car. In seconds, they were gone. Ann Brusselman never
looked back.

"Guess we better get out of here fast," Hank said. "We're the
only passengers left on this entire train."

Jack reached up and took the crutches out of the overhead
rack. "I'll need these." He started tearing the paper off. "Sure
hope we don't have any problems."

Hank Holt rubbed his hands together fiercely. "You bet.
Okay, kid. Let's move it."

The crutches helped Jack walk down the aisle. The trip down
the stairs proved to be another matter. Pain and the stretching
of the taut skin over the burned areas proved to be worse than
before. When he finally reached the cement walkway, Jack had
to lean on the crutches to keep from falling forward.

"How bad is it?" Hank asked.

"I'm bleeding."

"It's some distance to the other end." Hank started looking
around the huge terminal. "Can you walk okay?"

"I have to!" Jack gritted his teeth. "Let's get going." He swung the crutches around and started walking stiffly. The dimness of the night covered the entire area in shadows.

"I'll keep hold of your arm." Hank slipped his hand under Jack's elbow. "Let me know if you need more support."

Jack nodded and kept struggling on.

At the far end of the tracks where the walkways converged, a row of turnstiles provided an exit for all passengers. A surge of people hurried toward the metal egress that only allowed people to exit.

"We're going to have to merge with those people," Hank said.

"And I don't see any single women standing around." Jack stopped and peered into the dimness. "Wonder if something happened?"

"I guess we don't have any choice but to plow ahead." Hank took hold of his arm more firmly. "You just get through those turning doors anyway you can."

Jack began his persistent shuffle, trying to blend into the crowd without getting knocked over. When he came to the turnstile, Jack edged in and hobbled around as fast as he could. Moments later Hank came through the adjacent door.

"You got through okay?" Hank whispered.

Jack nodded and took a deep breath. "Trouble is that I don't see anybody looking for us." He pointed to the far front door of the terminal. "Look! That's a German soldier out there."

"Let's step out of the way," Hank said. "I don't think we have any choice except to wait for someone to show."

"Jean!" A small, brown-haired young woman abruptly jumped out of the crowd and hugged Jack. "So good to see you! And this must be your friend Henri!" She smiled broadly.

Both men stared in consternation.

"Henri, I am Monique. Monique Sernin." She shook his hand warmly. "Well, Jean, I have a car waiting for us outside. Let's go." She slipped her arm behind the crutches and into his. "Just one big happy family."

Walking at a painfully slow pace, they crossed the expansive corridor lined with little shops and walked out onto the street, still crowded at this hour of night.

"Paris never sleeps," Monique chattered happily. "Life's always at a buzz on our boulevards. Why don't we walk down the street a bit and stand on the corner to watch the cars."

When they reached the turn, Monique pushed them back into the shadows. Her smile vanished and a hard look crossed her eyes.

"Listen *carefully*. In five minutes exactly, I will pull up to this corner. You be there and jump in my car. Understand?"

"Sure," Hank said.

Monique paused for a moment, looked carefully up and down the street, then turned and disappeared into the night.

The men hovered against the stone building and waited. Exactly five minutes later, Monique pulled up to the curb and pushed the door open. The Americans scrambled to get in her car and they pulled away into the night.

"They may be following us." Monique kept looking in her

rearview mirror. "You can't tell. The Gestapo might have been after you all the way from Brussels."

"You're kidding!" Hank gasped.

"This is no kiddies game," Monique shot back. "The Nazis slither around in ways you wouldn't imagine. Now listen closely. In a few minutes, I'm going to pull up to the subway. You will get out instantly and go down the steps. I'll park and join you later. We'll take the tube from here."

"What if you don't come back?" Jack asked.

"Then you boys are strictly on your own."

Without street lights, the entire block settled into darkness. Regardless of Monique Sernin's casual talk about a town that never slept, this section of Paris appeared abandoned and dead. Monique's car sped down the block and whirled up to the curb.

"Get out quickly," she ordered. "Wait for me at the bottom of the stairs." She pointed to a signpost. "The subway's down there." The door had barely slammed behind Jack when the car shot away.

"She didn't waste any time," Jack told Hank. "That woman moves faster than a whip."

Hank glanced around the dark street. "Feels like we've been abandoned in the middle of nowhere."

"I shutter at the thought of going down those stairs." Jack pointed toward the entrance to the subway. "That hole in the sidewalk looks like a descent into a tomb."

"Let's get after it before Monique comes back." Hank took hold of Jack's arm. "It'll take us long enough anyway and will hurt you plenty. I'll help you get down."

The two men trudged toward the steps. Suddenly two men in felt hats and overcoats rushed up from the bottom and grabbed Hank and Jack.

"Stand still!" the first man warned in English. "We've got a gun trained on you. You'd be dead before you could turn around."

"Just like they told us!" the second man said. "One of you would be on crutches."

Hank raised his hands slowly and didn't speak.

The first man waved his outstretched hand back and forth, signaling a car. Headlights came on across the street and a German touring car made a U-turn across the middle of the street, swerving around to where they were standing. In seconds both Jack and Hank had been handcuffed.

"Don't even breathe a sound," the second man barked. "Get in that car and keep your mouths shut."

Sitting in the backseat sandwiched between their two captors, Jack and Hank stared straight ahead. They had a problem much graver than Monique had even indicated as possible. The Gestapo were about to haul them off.

The third man driving the car never looked around so it was impossible for Jack to know what he looked like. The two men who grabbed the Americans never spoke. In the darkness, Jack didn't get a good look at either person. No light had come on in the car so he didn't know anymore.

Jack agonized over what could have happened. Possibly the Gestapo had grabbed Reverend Assink and the Brusselmans. Maybe they'd already nabbed Monique Sernin. With their hands locked together in front of them, they were helpless. Jack began to recognize how much his legs were throbbing.

The touring car roared down the streets for fifteen minutes, turning corners sharply and winding through Paris like a deer on the run. Eventually they drove into an alley but didn't slow down. After they had gone down six alleys, the car pulled into an open garage in the middle of the block. The three abductors jerked Jack and Hank out of the car.

"Stay between us," the first man warned. "We're walking down a long dark corridor." He switched on a flashlight.

Without any more being said, the five men trudged through a narrow, dark hallway. The flashlight revealed nothing more than a rock floor. When they came to a big door, the first man said something in French through a hole in the thick wall. The large, heavy door slowly cracked open.

All Jack could see on the other side was the shadow of an enormous man. Without saying a word, he pointed over his shoulder. The march started again. After fifty feet Jack and Hank realized they had walked into a small room.

"If you want to stay healthy, don't make any noise," the huge man growled. "We'll be back later."

The four men shut the door behind them. A key clicked in the lock, breaking the silence. Sounds of their heels clicking against the floor echoed down the hall before disappearing.

Finally Jack whispered. "Where are we?"

"Looks like some kind of a holding room." Hank walked cautiously forward, trying to feel any furniture. "Not much in here."

"Hey," Jack said far too loud. "I just bumped into a bed."

"Yeah and there's one over here."

"Got any idea what it looks like?" Jack asked.

"No. We're probably better off not seeing."

Jack sat down slowly. "My legs are killing me. At least I can stretch out."

"Must be around one o'clock," Hank concluded. "We might as well try to get some sleep."

Jack stretched out on the thin, narrow mattress. "Feels like it's paper thin, but at least it's a bunk."

"Think you can sleep?" Hank asked.

"After a day like this one?" Jack rubbed his eyes. "We've run our motors about as fast as they'll go. We got every reason to be dog tired."

Hank didn't answer. He'd probably already drifted off.

The sound of a key turning in the lock brought Jack straight up in bed. He blinked several times but the intense blackness revealed nothing. A flashlight shot into his face.

"Okay, gentlemen," a voice said in English, "time to arise."

Hank shifted in his bed. "Can you tell us what time it is."

"Seven o'clock in the morning," the man said.

"My, my," Hank quipped. "How time flies when you have nothing to do but lie on a thoroughly uncomfortable bed."

"Please follow me." The man gestured with the flashlight. "Stay close behind me."

Jack and Hank fell in and started down a long corridor. At the end, a door opened in front of them. A burst of brilliant light caused them to squint. Only after they had stood inside the room for a few moments did they realize it was normal sunlight. Three men sat around the room and a huge man stood behind a desk.

"We trust you had a good night's sleep," the enormous man said. "Permit me to introduce myself. I am Burnell Manville."

Jack took full measure of this man at least six-foot six-inches tall. With powerful shoulders and arms, Burnell Manville could well have been the featured strongman in a circus. His thick brown beard and black piercing eyes left a menacing impression. A straight nose between high cheekbones and a strong jaw gave the appearance of a man accustomed to being in charge.

"You probably aren't sure of what's going on," Manville continued. "Let me begin by introducing my assistant." He pushed a button on his desk.

Monique Sernin immediately entered the room.

"Monique!" Jack gasped.

"I'm sure you think the Gestapo nabbed her," Manville said. "Actually we wanted to run you through a process to make sure you were the real thing and we needed a little time to check out some reports we were receiving." He grinned. "You are in the central headquarters of the Comete Line in Paris. Welcome."

"The Comete Line!" Hank said. "Why I thought that—"

"Yes, yes," Manville broke in. "Our men are good at imitating the enemy." Manville winked. "They're not bad at killing them also." He shrugged. "But all things in due time. The first order of business is to give you a shower, feed you breakfast, and get you ready for the next step in the escape process." He crossed his thick brawny arms over his large chest. "You do understand this is dangerous business?"

"Are you kidding?" Hank shook his head. "We've nearly been killed a half dozen times already. Yeah. We've got that idea."

"Then you'll appreciate what I have to tell you," Monique said. "We have intercepted an inside report from Brussels. The Gestapo killed Dirk Vogel and Madame Somerville. We don't yet know what they learned. Maybe nothing, but we must assume some information was forced out of them. These executions have put a high price on your heads. We can take nothing for granted."

"I understand," Jack said. "Frankly, Hank and I are both concerned. All we want to do is get out of this country. We'll do whatever you tell us."

"We must make sure that Harold Assink and Madame Brusselman got back to Brussels without problems," Monique said. "Then we'll work out the next step."

"Do you mind if I ask exactly where we are?" Hank inquired.

"Sorry," Manville said. "You don't want to know anything about this setup. If you were captured, it would be important for you not to be tortured into divulging facts about us." He raised an eyebrow. "Always a possibility you know."

Jack nodded. "Sure."

"If you gentlemen will follow me," Monique said. "We have breakfast waiting." She led them out of the room.

CHAPTER SIXTEEN

*B*erg Heydrich sat behind his desk in the Brussels Gestapo office waiting for Arnwolf Mandel to arrive. Heydrich glanced at his watch. By 8:30 in the morning, every Gestapo agent should be in his office on the job. For some reason, no one, including Karl Herrick, seemed to know where Mandel was. Heydrich didn't like dilatoriness. He already considered Mandel inept, and now his tardiness only added to a bad impression.

A sharp knock on the door interrupted Heydrich's thoughts. "Enter!"

Arnwolf Mandel walked in. "*Heil* Hitler!" he nearly shouted and saluted.

"*Heil* Hitler," Heydrich answered in a perfunctory manner. "Please sit down," he said with rigid formality. "We've been trying to find you *all* morning." Heydrich's eyes narrowed. "No one had any idea where you were."

"Ah, yes!" Mandel blinked nervously. "I've been in Ghent." He gestured aimlessly. "I was following a lead that went nowhere."

Heydrich studied Mandel's face carefully. No question about it. The man was lying. "A lead? Can you give me the details?"

"Those two American pilots I'm chasing were rumored to be on the run in that direction. I was interested in the situation around the small towns of Melle and Laarne." He forced a smile.

Heydrich bounced his fingers together. "Humph!" He abruptly shuffled through papers on his desk. "My understanding is that all you got out of young Vogel . . . before you killed him . . . was that one of the men used crutches."

"Exactly. A problem of burns."

"The woman told you nothing more."

"Small woman," Mandel said. "But hard as cement. Unfortunately, she died before we got anything else out of her."

Berg Heydrich raised an eyebrow. "That's why we don't apply so much pressure so fast," he said in a superior tone. "Putting the knife in people tends to shorten their lives."

Mandel looked uncomfortable but didn't answer.

Heydrich pulled a report out of the stack of papers on his desk and turned to his intercom system. "Please send in Agent Meier."

Moments later a short, squatty man walked into the office. "Agent Meier reporting, sir." The man saluted.

"Thank you." Heydrich smiled pleasantly. "My understanding is that you were checking trains last night when two unusual men boarded."

"Yes, sir." The agent pulled out a small notebook and flipped through the pages. "Yes. Train 105 to Paris. Two men. One man could barely walk."

"Tell us more, Meier," Heydrich said and offered the man a cigarette. "Your experience is important."

Meier lit the cigarette. "The two men seemed to be together and were dressed something like laborers, but I noticed their hair-cuts weren't exactly like what we get around here. It caught my eye." He puffed on the cigarette. "The backs of their heads seemed to have been cut with more precision. Higher up their necks."

"And the man with the walking problem?" Heydrich asked.

The short man pursed his lips and squinted. "This tall man spoke to me in German but with a strange sound, a sort of foreign twist to the words. Didn't recognize the accent. His papers and photo were in order but I watched him carefully. He walked with a stiff-legged, swinging motion as if trying to avoid bending his knees."

Heydrich leaned forward. "Like maybe this good-sized man had burns on his legs?"

"Ah!" The short man grinned. "I believe you've put your finger on it. Yes. Exactly."

"Thank you, Agent Meier. You are most observant."

Meier beamed. "Thank you, *mein leiter.*" He saluted and walked out.

"From this report, I think Paris would be a better bet than Ghent," Heydrich said coldly. "I would suggest that you might want to take your search in that direction."

Mandel rubbed his chin nervously. "Yes. Definitely. Herrick and I will be on our way at once."

"I will have an agent assigned to meet you when you arrive in Paris. Go directly to our headquarters in France."

Mandel licked his lips with a quick jittery thrust. "Thank you, sir. We'll be on our way today." He flashed a quick smile and hurried out of the room.

Berg Heydrich watched the door close. This fat jerk from Maastrich was the sort of fellow that Heydrich hated—creepy little snake slithering around as if he were chasing chickens, and worth little more. The idiot should never have killed Vogel and the woman. In time, Heydrich's men would have gotten far more out of them. Mandel's impulsiveness simply rushed the interrogation process out of all proportion. The fool! Heydrich was certain Arnwolf Mandel had been lying to him. Probably Mandel was out chasing some woman in Ghent. Well, getting him on his way to Paris would keep Mandel out of the Brussels office and that was worth something.

Arnwolf Mandel walked quickly back to his office in the Gestapo headquarters in Brussels. He didn't like the conversation with Berg Heydrich; he liked even less the possibility that Heydrich might have discovered that he had been in Ghent with Arabella Kersten, his mistress.

Mandel shut the door behind him. Without question, it

had been his intention to get back from Ghent in plenty of time to be in the office before 8:00. He'd left the night before after they killed Vogel and the woman for a quick run to Kersten's apartment. Unfortunately, an Allied airplane had crashed close to the highway and that threw everything into turmoil. Traffic was backed up for kilometers and even with his credentials, Mandel couldn't get through any faster. Arnwolf buzzed the intercom to get Karl Herrick into his office. Moments later Herrick hurried in.

"Heydrich's been looking for you," Karl began almost before he got the door closed. "He's particularly agitated."

"Yes, yes," Arnwolf waved Herrick's comments away. "I've taken care of the problem. It seems the Americans took the train south last night. We are going to drive to Paris and will take the highway through Saint-Quentin and go straight into the heart of the city. You must arrange a flat for me to stay in. Before we leave, I want you to send a request to the Paris office indicating that we want all the information they have on possible escape routes of Allied prisoners seeking to reach England."

"Yes, sir."

"And tell them we are seeking two men. Allied pilots. One is probably on crutches or walks with a limp. Understand?"

"Absolutely, *mein leiter*. When do we leave?"

"We must be on the road in less that two hours."

"I'll be ready." Karl Herrick saluted and immediately hurried from the room.

For ten minutes, Arnwolf pulled papers off his desk and stacked them in his briefcase. After he had gathered all of the available data on the crash of the American bomber, he picked up his private telephone and dialed Ghent.

"Hello," a woman's voice answered in a vague distant tone.

"Arabella!" Arnwolf snapped.

"Ah, my love!" Arabella Kersten immediately switched into the low, burring sound Arnwolf knew well.

"You seemed rather amorphous." Arnwolf sounded suspicious.

"I never know who is calling, darling. Have to be cautious."

"Listen carefully, Arabella." Arnwolf lowered his voice. "We are going to Paris."

"Paris!" Arabella broke into jubilation. "Wonderful!"

"I want you to take the train and meet me at the Paris city terminal this evening. Travel through Lille and I will be waiting for you in a little café inside the terminal proper. Understand?"

"Oh yes! Will we be there long?"

"Bring clothes for at least several weeks. I will have an apartment arranged for you to stay in."

"My Arnwolf is always the most thoughtful man in the entire world," Arabella cooed.

"Remember! Everything about this trip is completely secret."

"Of course. I will see you tonight, my dear."

Arnwolf hung up. They would again be in another country entirely, making these arrangements even more acceptable.

Parisians paid absolutely no attention to mistresses anyway. The fact that no one, including Karl Herrick, knew of her coming made Arabella's arrival even more workable. Arabella could stay in his flat and no one would know the difference. Once again Arnwolf had made arrangements that suited his needs and interests. He always felt good when things worked out. Now he felt good.

The small room had the feel of being used as a kitchen for a couple of centuries. An ambiance of antiquity hung in the air with ancient smoke stains lining the walls around the open oven. A brick chimney ran far up to the roof way above them. Whitewashed walls had now become stained with many hand-prints and spills.

"More scrambled eggs?" Monique Sernin stood over the kitchen table, watching the two Americans eat. "I can cook some more."

"You fed us like a farmer preparing a turkey for Thanksgiving," Hank Holt said.

"Thanksgiving?" Monique frowned. "What is that?"

"In the United States near the end of November we have a special holiday for thanking the good Lord for our many blessings," Jack Martin explained. "It's a big national holiday where we eat turkey and gorge ourselves. Great time. The big day is coming up soon."

Monique shrugged. "Never heard of it. Of course, the French don't pay a great deal of attention to the Americans, you know."

"We don't know that much about the French either." Jack smiled. "I guess by the time we get out of this country that'll change."

"Indeed!" Monique nodded soberly. "The journey will not be easy."

"Easy? Hasn't been yet." Hank grinned a sly smile. "We haven't been on your average bargain basement tour of Europe."

The door opened and the towering figure of Burnell Manville filled the entrance. "I see Monique has fed you well," he said with a heavy French accent. "Good."

"Magnificently." Jack grinned. "King Louie's cooks couldn't have done better."

Manville sat down and leaned over the table. "Let me bring you up to date. We've been able to clarify a number of issues. Assink and Madame Brusselman had no problems getting back to Brussels. Julien Brusselman hasn't had any surprise visits from the Gestapo. Good signs."

"Delighted to hear that," Jack said. "I've worried about their children."

"Yvonne and Jacques are fine," Manville said. "Unfortunately, our source for information on the work of the Gestapo hasn't found out anything about Dirk Vogel and Madame Somerville except that they were killed." Manville shook his head and his eyes became hard. "Tortured to death." For a moment he looked down at the tabletop solemnly. "More than sad."

Silence settled over the room and no one spoke. Monique returned to the stove. Jack and Hank sat quietly, waiting for Burnell Manville to begin again.

"We must assume something or the other leaked out and we must get the two of you on your way quickly," Manville continued. "Our leadership committee has discussed the matter and believes that it is best for you two men to dye your hair black. A change of color will make you more difficult to identify on the road. Of course, we will exchange your clothing and give you a different street appearance."

"Sound like good ideas," Jack said. "Unfortunately, I can't hide the fact that my legs are badly burned. I'm afraid I can't do anything to keep me from limping or using crutches."

"A problem!" Manville growled. "Yes, a significant problem. For this reason I will be traveling with you, as will Monique."

Monique turned around quickly. "Me? I didn't expect to—"

"The committee's decision," Manville said. "They feel we should leave today."

Monique blinked several times. "Of course, I am at their disposal."

"As we all are," Manville added sardonically. "I believe we should leave in at least one hour."

"One hour?" Jack bolted back in his chair. "That's not wasting any time."

"Of course!" Manville poked with his large index finger. "Our goal is to get you up to the *Pas de Calais*, the Strait of Dover, or as the English call it, the English Channel. As the crow flies, the distance isn't that great from Paris. Unfortunately, crows get shot down these days by Nazi Messerschmitts. The task is not easy and will demand considerable walking." He raised an eyebrow. "You up for hiking, Martin?"

Jack took a deep breath. "I will do whatever is demanded of me, sir."

"Good!" Manville smiled broadly. "Excellent attitude. I like your spirit." He slapped Jack on the back, giving him a jolt that nearly sent him out of his chair. "We'll do fine together."

"You really mean *an hour?*" Hank asked. "How soon will we actually leave?"

"As quickly as you've got black hair." Manville grinned. "Monique will give you her famous dye treatment. Good luck, boys." Burnell Manville roared with laughter and walked out. "Good luck indeed!" he called over his shoulder.

After finishing breakfast and changing clothing, Jack and Hank stepped out of the tall building into an inner courtyard where Burnell and Monique awaited them. The sky had taken on a cloudy overcast, throwing a distinct gray shadow over the city. In the center of the courtyard, a large Mercedes touring car waited on the cement driveway. A man in a brown coat with a red scarf stood by the car.

"Meet our driver," Manville said. "Carlo Roche has been one of our men from the beginning."

Jack and Hank both shook hands.

"My, my!" Manville said. "Our Americans have turned into Parisians!"

Jack shrugged. "We look bad?"

"No, no!" Manville said. "With your beret, your slightly used street coat, and those worn slacks, you have the look of the average Parisian artist strolling down the street looking for an outdoor café and a cup of coffee."

"And the hair?" Hank raised an eyebrow. "You're sure that's not a little much?"

"He doesn't like the color," Monique said. "Too black."

"Come now, come now," Manville chuckled. "Any actor at the *Folies* would be pleased."

"I feel rather obvious," Jack said. "I guess I'm not."

"All we have to deceive is the Gestapo," Manville said. "I think you will do fine. We have ... shall we say ... *acquired* a large vehicle to take us out of town. Shouldn't be any problem getting out of Paris. It's out there in the rolling fields where we'll have to be careful."

"What's our plan?" Jack asked.

"Carlo Roche will take us toward the town of Elbeuf on the Northwest side of France. We'll double back around toward the city of Arras. From there we'll have to start working our way through the German infantry. Nazi soldiers will be everywhere."

"I understand." Jack jutted his chin forward. "We are prepared for problems."

"Problems?" Manville snorted. *"Oh yes, we will have prob-lems. Let's be on our way."*

Without saying a word, Carlo Roche got in the car be-hind the wheel. Manville filled up the rest of the front seat. Monique Sernin and the Americans slipped into the backseat. The Mercedes sped out of the courtyard, through a narrow en-tryway and was suddenly on one of the Parisian avenues.

Jack watched people hurrying up and down the streets of the great city. The gray sky matched the resolute look on the people's faces. An atmosphere of quiet resignation hung in the eyes of citizens standing on the street corners, the look of a captured people. The Mercedes sped on toward the edge of the city without the driver speaking.

As the city of Paris disappeared behind them, Jack Martin could feel the skin on his shins tightening. He tried to say little about the pain, but his legs hurt most of the time. The con-stant throbbing worried Martin. The fact was that walking long distances would be almost impossible and Manville had made it clear they would have to do so. Jack tightened his jaw. No matter what happened, a struggle lay ahead of him.

Despair wrapped cold fingers around his neck as it had done the afternoon he stood on Ann Brusselman's terrace. Jack could almost physically feel hope drain out of his body. The task ahead of him didn't seem possible to accomplish.

An old memory returned from another one of those times when his grandfather laid out his same familiar line. Jack could see himself playing in front of their house on the dry, sun-baked prairie surrounding their Texas home. Drought had turned the grass into dried-up, worn stubble. Winds that could turn any daylight into a dust-filled foggy night howled around him. His father sat up on the porch holding his head between his hands. Granddad Hennie Matthys sat on the other side of him talking with great animation. Jack could hear them and knew that his father was in despair.

Staying around when all the other farmers were moving away didn't seem to make good sense. Jones down the road had already left for California, and the Brantleys, living in the farm on the other side of their back forty, talked of moving on to Arizona. Folks in town at the country store all said the same thing. There was no future left for the farmer in Texas. The Great Depression had swallowed all promise.

Jack could hear his grandfather's persistent preaching at his father. In his heavy German accent, Hennie kept saying over and over that endurance remained paramount. If they'd stay with the struggle, in time the Martin family would come out the other side and they'd make it financially. Hennie was sure of it.

"Keep on working, son," the old man insisted. "Another good day will yet dawn."

Driving across the French countryside, Jack could depend on nothing else but the old man's advice. If Granddad Hennie wasn't right, then he had no hope. Endurance remained paramount at this moment as much as it had a decade ago.

CHAPTER SEVENTEEN

The Mercedes touring car pulled off the highway and turned down a well-worn dirt road. After a couple of kilometers, the car stopped in front of an old stone farmhouse surrounded by tall trees with a rickety truck parked in the back. Jack Martin got out of the car and stretched. The burned areas on his legs still ached and it felt like his skin was drawing up.

"Looks like we've joined the bargain basement tour of Europe," Hank Holt whispered. "But I got to admit I like that car. Great ride."

"Sure, if you don't have any burns."

Burnell Manville's towering figure rolled out of the front seat and Monique Sernin eased out of the back before Carlo Roche turned the car around and roared back in the direction they had come.

"Our home away from home?" Jack asked.

"A little reprieve for the night," Manville answered. "Not much but it'll do for the evening."

Monique shaded her eyes with her hand and studied the terrain. "No sign of the Germans," she concluded. "Don't see any military trucks. Good news there."

"Ah, they're always around," Manville grumbled. "Probably will show up tonight. We must be ready."

"And how do we get ready?" Jack asked.

Manville looked at his watch. "Gonna be dark before long. We'll put you boys up in the attic without a light. Farm clothes are stored up there and you can change. That'll get you prepared. You're about to go from being men of Paris to country boys."

"Yeah," Hank said. "I'm good as long as I don't have to say anything."

"Martin can do the talking if necessary," Manville said. "Since he speaks German, you're in good order."

"We should go inside before someone sees us," Monique said. "We'll have to start early in the morning and the journey will demand walking. I imagine you will want to have a good night's sleep."

"Oh yeah," Jack grumbled.

The foursome walked inside the abandoned farmhouse. The kitchen looked like it might be a hundred years old but still appeared functional. Jack and Hank sat down around a battered dining table.

"Where'd the farmers go?" Jack asked.

Monique looked at Burnell and waited for him to explain. Her face became hard and her eyes flashed. "Go ahead. Tell 'em."

"What can I say," Burnell gestured aimlessly. "We all know what the Germans are capable of doing. Much like what happened in Belgium with Dirk Vogel." He stopped and took a deep breath. "They caught members of the family working in the underground for the Comete Line." He stopped and a deep sadness settled around his eyes. "They killed everybody in the family to teach the farmers in the area a lesson." Burnell shook his head. "Left an empty house behind. Some lesson, huh?"

Jack exchanged a glance with Hank, but nothing more was said. The French partisans left the room. After several minutes, the two Americans went upstairs and crawled up into the attic on a rickety ladder. The final tier of the house turned out to be floored with two straw mattresses lying in the center of the room. White shirts and work pants hung on nails driven into the beams supporting the roof. The floors had been swept recently enough that the attic proved to be a clean, although spartan, bedroom. The two men changed clothes and once again looked like farmers.

By the time darkness had fallen across the countryside, Monique had prepared a small supper of sausages and fried potatoes. The Americans ate without saying much.

"I suppose our little repast doesn't compare well with the cooking of Madame Brusselman?" Manville asked. "Huh?"

"We are pleased to have anything to eat," Jack said. "We could be out there in the field chewing on the grass."

Manville nodded. "Good perspective! You're right. I hope our trip doesn't descend to such a level."

Jack grinned. "We'll take whatever comes along. We appreciate having you as our friends."

Manville nodded his head. "This man is another Franklin Roosevelt—always ready with a quick, good answer. I like him." He slapped Jack briskly on the back. Jack groaned.

Jack and Hank finished supper and joked for a bit before closing up shop for the day. Only then did Jack fully realize how tired he was from the tension they had lived with while fleeing Paris.

"I guess it's time for us to turn in," Jack finally said. "Feeling a tad tired."

"Yes," Monique said. "Our work is stressful. Sleep well. The night will seem short."

"Thank you." Jack stood up. "Please call us if we're not down here by morning."

"But don't come down if we are raided by the Germans," Manville said. "Only if we call you."

"Don't worry," Hank said. "We're not anticipating any conversations with the Krauts."

The two men returned to the attic, pulling the ladder up behind them. Darkness became as thick as a blanket, surrounding them with nothing but a few strange shapes protruding through the blackness. They closed the flat attic door and locked it.

"Ah, nothing like a quiet evening in France," Hank said through the blackness. "Relaxing under a starlit sky with the Seine River rippling past and filling our heads with romantic notions. Is that what you say, Jack, old boy?"

"I don't find a dusty attic filled with a couple of piles of hay to be my idea of a pleasant jaunt through the French countryside. No, this isn't my idea of good times."

For a long time the two men lay in the darkness, staring up at the vague forms of the beams overhead. The strong scent of hay filled their noses with an unpleasant dryness. Hiding in an attic while Germans with rifles could possibly be surrounding the house had its own foreboding aura.

"Why are we doing this?" Hank abruptly said.

"Why? Because Uncle Sam sent us an engraved invitation to join the party. That's why!"

"No, I mean what is it that we're fighting about? Sometimes when I'm in one of these bizarre situations I have to remind myself why in the world I am on this grind."

Jack rolled over. "Are you serious?"

"Sorta. I'd like your thoughts."

"The Nazis killed Dirk Vogel and an innocent woman in Brussels who wanted to do nothing more than help frightened, fleeing soldiers. Germans murdered the farmers who lived in this farmhouse after they invaded their country. Someone might call these swine Gestapo policemen, but I'd call them butchers. We're out here fighting this war to stop the Fascist tyranny from ruling the world with fear and intimidation. I think that makes sleeping in an old attic worthwhile."

After several moments Hank answered. "Yeah. You got it. I think that's worth the trip up the rickety ladder."

The two men rolled over and went to sleep.

The first light of dawn broke through the thatched roof, scattering small rays of sunlight over the attic. Jack stirred and rubbed his eyes. Even though the night had been long enough, he wasn't ready to get up and start the long walk waiting before them. Carefully extending his toes downward, Jack tried to loosen the skin on his shins. For several minutes he rotated his ankles and tried to rub his legs. Only then did Jack get out of the straw mattress and start walking slowly around the attic. Eventually the pain eased some and it became easier to walk faster.

Hank rolled over and watched him make the fourth turn around the flat floor. "You must enjoy walking so much that you just have to start before any of the rest of us even get out of the sack."

Jack didn't say anything but kept walking.

"What a runner," Hank continued jabbing at him. "Never saw anything finer than a Texas boy beating it out on an indoor French track. Brings tears to my eyes."

Jack eyed him menacingly. "How'd you like me to bring blood to your nose?"

"See. There you go messing up all the touching aura surrounding this trot."

Jack kept walking.

"I imagine Man Mountain Manville's already up." Hank stood up. "He doesn't seem to miss a lick."

Jack slowed down and started putting the work clothes on.

"I've got a feeling that it's going to be a long day. I need to be loosened up as much as I can."

"Yeah," Hank's countenance changed. "I'm sure you're right. This will be a tough one." He started putting on an identical set of white attire.

The sound of someone poking on the attic door signaled it was time to come down. The two men unlocked the door and stuck the old ladder down. Quickly descending, they walked down the stairs into the kitchen.

Jack stopped and stared at two strange men sitting at the dining table drinking coffee with Burnell Manville. "Didn't know . . ." He kept staring.

"No problem," Manville said. "They're part of our crew. Meet Eliot Etienne and his brother Gano."

"*Avec plaisir*," Jack said.

The men shook hands but didn't speak.

"They're going with us?" Hank asked.

Manville nodded his head. "We will look like five simple farm boys heading off to the fields. If we don't run into the Germans, we'll keep walking."

"And if we do?" Jack asked.

Manville grinned. "Who knows?" he chuckled. "Could prove interesting."

The two Americans sat down and started eating the hot mush Monique had laid out for them along with a slice of hard bread. Jack looked around and didn't see the woman.

"Where's Monique?" Jack asked.

"Out doing a little task for you," Manville said. "You'll see." He wiggled his thick eyebrows.

Jack had learned that when the huge man didn't explain a response, it was best to drop the question. They ate silently until the back door opened and the French woman came in carrying two long wooden sticks. Monique had changed into pants and a shirt that made her look like one of the men. With her hair pulled up under a small black cap, Monique looked like any other farm boy.

"See!" Manville pointed. "What did I tell you?"

Monique thrust the small wooden branches into Jack's hands. "I cut these off the trees outside. The Y-shape at the top will fit under your arms. We can't afford for the Germans to see you out here in the country with commercial crutches. You can trim the length to fit you."

Jack stared. "Well, my gosh! Great idea. I'll look even more like the local scene."

Manville stood up. "I don't want to rush you gentlemen, but we need to start our little stroll. We're going to cut through the fields and ramble down the road. After we've been walking awhile, Monique will start the truck waiting in back. If we don't run into problems, she'll come along and pick us up." He looked at the French woman. "Right?"

"Unless I hear shooting," she said. "Then, I'll come much faster."

"As soon as Jack has his crutches adjusted, we're off." Manville pointed toward the door. "Ready?"

Eliot and Gano Etienne still did not speak. Almost without making a sound, they got up and walked out. Within a few minutes, Jack had the crutches cut to a length to fit him.

"I can walk some of the time without them," Jack said. "They'll help enormously if I get tired or start having pain."

Monique nodded but said nothing. The alluring feminine appearance Jack had seen when she first greeted them at the train station had disappeared and only a plain-faced boyish worker stood in front of him. In a matter of minutes everything had changed.

For forty-five minutes Manville led his crew of four men across the open pasture. Jack started off at a good pace, but the field proved to be soft and filled with thick weeds, causing him to stumble. When his feet sank into the moist ground, walking became even more difficult. In twenty minutes Jack was using the stick crutches Monique had made for him. While he didn't say anything, the end of the sticks that fit under his arms turned out to be hard and when he nearly tripped, the wood pressed harshly against his armpits and sank into the ground. When they reached the edge of the field and came to a rock fence, Jack knew his dread of the long hike had been an understatement. The short walk had already proved to be more difficult than he had anticipated.

"The road is on the other side of the rock wall," Manville said. "We're getting close to what might turn out to be a German checkpoint. Pay close attention."

Eliot and Gano Etienne nodded, but didn't speak.

"What's that mean for us?" Hank asked.

Manville shrugged. "Hard to say. Maybe nothing. Depends on what the enemies do."

"Like?" Hank pressed.

"We'll see." Manville retreated into his silent mode and sprang over the fence.

Jack found it difficult to clear the rock fence. He had to sit in the middle of the sharp points and swing his legs over one at a time. Hobbling through the grass and down the slope to the road, he fixed his crutches under his armpits again. While the road was dirt, the surface felt more secure than the field.

Manville looked at Eliot and Gano with a hard glare before jabbering something in French that neither Jack or Hank understood. The Étienne brothers nodded, remaining silent. The three men started down the road with Jack and Hank bringing up the rear.

"Get the feeling that we're a bit on the outside of things?" Hank quipped under his breath.

Jack smiled. "They're doing it all for us."

"Yeah, but I'd like to know what's going on."

"Hang in there. We'll find out soon enough."

When the men reached the end of the field, Manville nodded to the right and they turned. Once they had cleared a slight hill, Jack saw soldiers ahead of him. It looked like three Germans were standing with rifles on their shoulders while a fourth man sat behind a machine gun. Barbed wire had been strung across the road behind the Germans to stop any vehicle.

Manville didn't slacken the pace. The three Frenchmen kept their steady gait. Hank slipped behind them and Jack brought up the rear.

The Y of Jack's crutches kept digging into his armpits and he wanted to stop, but he knew they couldn't even slow down. Two of the German soldiers took their rifles off their shoulders but Manville's company of four maintained their pace. As they got closer, Jack realized the Germans were more the age of boys.

Manville waved. *"Hallo!"*

Although they looked menacing, the Germans seemed indifferent. No one cocked a rifle. The soldiers only looked at the farmers as if they were the usual peasants who traveled the roads daily.

"Verzeichnis!" The first German held out his hands.

Manville smiled and saluted. He turned to the brothers standing around him and held up two fingers. The three men reached into their coats and pockets.

In a flash, Manville and the Etienne brothers whipped out pistols and started firing rapidly. A fifth Nazi soldier popped out of the bushes and Manville shot him through the head. In a matter of seconds, they had killed the boy soldiers before even one of them had gotten off a shot.

Jack and Hank stood dazed. The shooting had occurred so quickly they didn't even have an opportunity to drop to the road to protect themselves from flying bullets. Both Americans stared in shock.

"Y-you k-killed them," Jack sputtered.

"You wanted to shake hands?" Manville growled. "We're not exactly on a first name basis with our enemies."

The Etienne brothers rushed at the dead soldiers and jerked off their rifles and pistols. Eliot and Gano pressed two Lugers into the Americans' hands.

"Next time you can shoot too," Manville said.

Jack stared at the weapon. Americans considered the Luger a top-of-the-line pistol. Here he was holding one.

"If they catch you with the Luger, they'll kill you with it," Manville added. "You need to go down shooting."

Jack nodded and swallowed hard. "Why'd you hold up two fingers?"

"That's our signal," Manville said. "Means 'come shooting!'" He winked. "Effective. Huh?"

The roar of the old truck echoed off in the distance. Monique was on her way. Without anything being said, the Etienne brothers quickly cleared the barbed wire off the roads. Manville pulled the German soldier from behind the machine gun and pushed him into the bushes. Hank started dragging the other two soldiers out of the way, pulling them into the ditch. Jack leaned on his crutches and watched in horrified bewilderment.

By the time the truck chugged up the road, the men had cleared all the Nazi debris out of the way, leaving an appearance of an empty open road.

"Everybody all right?" Monique asked, leaning out the window of the truck.

Manville shrugged. "We are. They aren't." He hurried around to the back of the truck and pushed the machine gun in. "Hurry up and get in the back. We need to get out of here."

"Couldn't we run into more Germans?" Jack asked.

"Not likely for a while," Manville answered. "We knew the Nazis were here, but I don't think we'll find any more ahead of us for some time."

"Knew they were here?" Jack's voice raised. "And you didn't tell us?"

"Surprise tends to make you act natural," Manville said. "A little fear in your eyes helps."

Jack's mouth dropped.

"Get in the truck, Yank," Manville said. "We're going to give you a little break. Get you off your feet." The big man chuckled. "We're better guys than you gentlemen think."

Jack edged up on the bed of the truck without knowing what to say. The rickety truck fired up again and bumped down the road with Manville sitting in the front seat and the Etienne brothers with the Americans in the back. Jack stared in astonishment out the back of the slow-moving truck.

He had lost count of how many times a brush with death had nearly cost his life. Crashing the bomber, hiding in the Sambre Meuse River, fever at the Brusselman's, walking within feet of the Nazis before he knew the Germans were about to die; the list felt endless. Jack's head swirled and his heart pounded.

Had it gotten easier to look death in the eye? Not by the width of a hair! His stomach still knotted and he felt slightly nauseated. Jack swore to himself that if they survived this trek, he'd never mention the experience to anyone.

CHAPTER EIGHTEEN

Chez Bourges had never been the most elegant bistro in Paris. Not far from the Hotel de Soubise, the restaurant remained too secluded to attract the big-money customers. Still, Chez Bourges was more than enough to impress Arabella Kersten. Arnwolf Mandel had a sense of these things and knew how to spend as little as possible to get the most for his francs. Bringing Arabella to Paris had not been an impulsive decision. Arnwolf had considered the idea several times in the past, but now that he had been assigned to an office in the famous city, the pieces fit. If someone recognized a woman was with him, it would make no difference. The French never mentioned such things.

"I love this *gastsatte*," Arabella cooed and toasted Arnwolf with a glass of champagne.

"*Bistro*," Arnwolf corrected her and drank the bubbly.

"Whatever. You know how to show a girl a good time."

Arnwolf grinned. "You know how to show a boy a good time."

Arabella giggled. "Silly boy." She winked. "I always wanted to come to Paris. Of course, I never got far beyond Ghent. This trip is one big step for me."

"You will find Paris filled with magnificent creations. Perhaps, we will find time tomorrow to visit the Louvre. Paintings are excellent." He raised an eyebrow. "Of course, Berlin has better."

The fact Arnwolf Mandel had never been to the Louvre or any other gallery in Berlin meant nothing. A museum was cheaper than shopping. He considered deception to be part of his stock in trade. Arabella Kersten was too dumb and limited to know the difference. He considered her to be little more than entertainment. Certainly not equal to his stature.

Having finished with the lobster, Arnwolf lit a cigarette and sipped the white wine that came with the main course. "Care for a smoke?"

"Please," Arabella said. "Your cigarettes are excellent."

Arnwolf smiled. "Being the victor in battle always has consequences for Germany. The Gestapo is able to obtain the best. One of the attributes of our profession."

"Tell me about your work in Paris," Arabella said. "I'd like to know more about what you do while we are here."

"Top secret." Arnwolf shrugged. "Part of the job."

"Hmm, sounds mysterious."

"Very." Arnwolf took on the air of superiority that he hoped enhanced his appearance. "But I am running down Allied pilots."

"Something big must be going on in Paris."

"Perhaps."

"See!" Arabella giggled again. "I knew it. You're always working at something or other behind the scenes."

Arnwolf stiffened. Across the room he recognized Karl
Herrick talking to a waiter. He had told Herrick where he'd
be but warned Herrick he wanted no interruptions. Whatever
brought the aide to this bistro had better be more than good.
The waiter pointed to Arnwolf's table and Herrick walked
quickly toward them.

Herrick clicked his heels and bowed his head subserviently.
"Please excuse the interruption." He stared at Arabella.

"What is it?" Arnwolf sounded distant and irritated.

"I have some unexpected information that I felt you would
want to receive immediately."

"I trust it is urgent."

"Yes, sir." Herrick smiled at Arabella in a perfunctory manner. "I believe it is also confidential."

Arnwolf pushed back from the table. "Sorry, my dear. I'll be
back shortly."

The two men left the table and walked toward the front
door. Once they were outside, Arnwolf leaned into his aide's
face. "This better be important."

"A report came in only minutes ago, sir. The *Wehrmacht*
found four of their soldiers shot on a country road out there
between Elbeuf and Arras, towns on the northwest side of
France. Not far away, they found a farmhouse where parti-
san insurgents were caught and killed several weeks ago. In

investigating the shootings, it was discovered that a truck had been stolen from the farmhouse. When I read the report, I thought it sounded like the Americans at work."

Arnwolf rubbed his chin. "That's the direction prisoners might take in trying to flee the country."

Karl Herrick nodded his head.

"It fits. Those swine are making a run for the English Channel. We must leave immediately."

"Yes, sir," Herrick said.

"Stay here." Arnwolf opened the door and hurried back into the restaurant.

Arabella still sat sipping wine and gawking around the restaurant as if she might see someone of significance. The sparkle remained in her eyes.

"I have unfortunate news," Arnwolf said, sitting down. "I must leave at once."

"A-at o-once?"

"Immediately. Hopefully my prey is near at hand. Please go back to the hotel by yourself and stay there until I return."

"*By myself!*" Arabella's eyes flashed. "You're kidding! We came here for a big party."

Arnwolf placed money on the table. "Pay the bill and I hope to see you soon. Wait for my telephone call."

"But . . ." Arabella tossed her napkin on the table. "You said this was going to be one big party."

"Stay in the hotel." Arnwolf turned and marched out of the restaurant without looking back.

Extremely tall Lombardy poplars lined the side of the farm property, sheltering the stone house beneath their long shadows. At the back of the front yard, the door to an animal pen swung back and forth, conveying the message of emptiness. The sun had gone down when the truck stopped beside the abandoned farmhouse.

Burnell Manville and his men climbed out of the truck and stretched. The Americans inched out of the back more carefully.

"How's your legs?" Hank Holt asked.

"Better than they would have been if we had walked all day," Jack said. "Little on the stiff side."

"Got any idea where we are?" Hank looked around the yard. "This farm's sure seen better days. Looks abandoned."

"Maybe this is another one of those cozy spots where the Germans stopped in to teach somebody a lesson."

"Hope not," Hank said.

Burnell Manville walked around the side of the truck. "Looks like you gentlemen had a decent ride. Feel in acceptable condition?"

"Beats walking," Jack grinned. "No, sir. No complaints out of me."

"I've got one question for you," Hank said. "We appreciate the fact the Comete Line is hustling us out of the country and back to our fighting units. There's no way we can express how much we value what you and the Etienne brothers did today." He held up one finger. "But I've got one question. Why can't you let us in on where we are going?"

Manville shrugged. "You want the truth, huh?"

"I think it would help us know what's happening," Jack added.

"And that's what we don't want you to do." Manville shook his head vigorously. "We want you to hobble along like ordinary country boys who have no idea what's going to happen. We've found it makes it easier to fool the Germans." Manville held up two fingers. "Second. We could get captured. If the Nazis got us, you couldn't be tortured into telling them anything."

"I see your point," Jack said. "Just worries us not to know where we're headed."

"Home," Manville winked. "We'll get you there."

"Okay," Hank said. "Can you give us a hint where we've been today and are tonight?"

"Sure. We're not far from the border with Belgium near the town of Arras. We've been traveling due north of Paris in a zigzag fashion, winding back and forth over the country roads so that it would be hard to follow us. There are a thousand of these backcountry roads that the farmers use. Makes it hard to identify us as anything but peasants." He shook his finger like a school teacher. "Make no mistake about it! We've been driving in the midst of the *Wehrmacht*. Just haven't seen any of 'em yet."

"Other than the boys we killed this morning."

"Well!" Manville grinned. "We knew they were there. Them boys were our point of passage into the territory where the Germans are the strongest."

"Then they have missed them by now?" Hank asked.

"Long before now," Manville said. "I'm sure they figured the soldiers were gone well before noon."

"Hmm." Jack pursed his lips. "Then they must be after us."

"I'd say that's an accurate conclusion," Manville said. "That's another reason we've been doubling back and forth. Got to give them Germans something to think about."

"Yeah," Hank said. "I'm sure they're thinking it over right now."

"We'll be doing some back pedaling in the morning." Manville pointed over his shoulder. "Going south to Amiens. Lots of Nazi soldiers down there."

"Supper will be ready soon!" Monique Sernin shouted from the house. "There's a well out back. Wash your hands."

"House is a little sparse," Manville said. "Shouldn't be a problem with the Nazis tonight. Then again, you never know."

Burnell Manville's selection of sleeping quarters proved to have thin walls. Wind whistled through the cracks causing the Comete Line escape crew to sleep with blankets pulled over their heads to preserve all the warmth possible. Ancient by American standards, the old ceiling had fallen on the old farmhouse, exposing bare wooden beams. Leaves and debris lay littered across the broken floor. Obviously, no one had been in the house for some time. In such chambers, cold November nights had their own unique way of cutting to the bone, and no one wanted to push his luck. The sun had started coming up later as the month passed and everyone slept until the sky started becoming gray. As always seemed to be the case, Burnell Manville was the first one up, lumbering around the room like a cranky bull and making it impossible for everyone else to sleep.

While he didn't want to be the last one out of the sack, Jack Martin found his legs stiff and nearly immobile. Extra walking hadn't been long the day before, but it took a toll. As he did every morning, Jack stretched his toes, rubbed his shins and tried to get the circulation moving. No matter what he did, nothing removed the pain and stiffness easily.

"When are we going to eat?" Manville roared.

Monique Sernin glared at him. "You want to fix the breakfast?"

"How about some eggs?" Manville barked back.

"Go out and find them. I didn't notice any chickens flying around when we showed up last night. You got a magic touch?"

"Humph!" Manville growled. "I need something hot."

"Build a fire." Monique didn't give an inch. "I've got plenty to do myself."

Manville stomped around the kitchen and grumbled under his breath.

Jack ignored the skirmish. He'd already noticed that the longer they traveled the more Monique and Burnell argued.

Jack had gotten used to the fact that the Etienne brothers said nothing most of the time, except to themselves. Hank Holt remained his main source of conversation.

When Jack looked for his friend, he discovered Hank was gone. Without saying anything, Jack stiffly started rolling up his blankets. Eventually Hank came in from the outside and sat down by him.

"Cold out there," Hank said. "Looks like it'll snow today."

"That's all we need is a snowstorm," Jack said.

"Won't pile up," Manville interrupted them from behind. "I got the report from the BBC. Cold but no big buildup is expected."

"Good," Jack said. "I'm not big on blizzards."

"Want to give us any hints where we're going today?" Hank asked the big man.

"Sure." Manville shrugged. "Won't make any difference today. As soon as we eat, we'll head south for the town of Amiens. Lots of Germans there. Going backward into a nest of the enemy is a tactic meant to confuse anyone who might be chasing us."

"Really think somebody is after us?" Jack said.

"We always assume the worst," Manville answered. "If it doesn't happen, so much the better." He walked toward the kitchen. "If bad happens, we're prepared."

The entire crew quickly disassembled their equipment and ate a cold breakfast of salami and hunks of bread washed down with cold water. No one wanted to start a fire and chance sending up smoke. As soon as they were through, Manville and the Etienne brothers started hiding the machine gun on the underside of their old truck. In a short time, the truck was completely loaded and Jack crawled in the open back end.

The temperature hadn't risen and he pulled one of the blankets over him. Little was said as they rumbled out of the farmyard and started south. Heavy flakes of snow drifted through the air and settled on the bed of the truck. Jack immediately realized it was even colder than he thought, forcing him and Hank to huddle together. His fingers throbbed and his toes hurt, but he knew that nothing should be said about the discomfort. Eliot and Gano Etienne sat stoically in front of him, apparently oblivious to the bitter cold wind whipping into the truck. The men bounced back and forth while the driver tried to avoid the potholes in the dirt road.

Jack's teeth started chattering and he pulled the blanket closer around his neck. Numbness started creeping up his feet and hands. He knew that something must get his mind off the biting cold that might yet freeze his nose. Jack ducked under the covers and put his arm over his mouth and nose to keep some warmth around his face.

In the darkness of the covering, Jack thought about home and how his parents must be doing. Thanksgiving would be here soon and they'd gather around the table and pray for him. Mom would weep and Dad would attempt to keep the feast jovial. He would fail. They would miss him as much as he missed them.

"Oh Lord," Jack prayed in a whisper. "It's cold. Please let the warmth of my parents' home surround us in some way. Sure don't want to freeze. We want out of here but we aren't going to make it without Your help. Be mighty nice for You to keep Your hand over this truck. Thank You, Sir. Amen."

The truck bounced off the dirt road and onto the highway. Amiens remained a long way away.

CHAPTER NINETEEN

Snow had already fallen over most of Amiens by the time Karl Herrick drove Arnwolf Mandel's Mercedes into the city. Herrick toured around for several minutes, giving Mandel some sense of the streets, but returned to the city square framed between a large cathedral and the ornate town hall where he found a parking place. Everywhere they looked, truckloads of soldiers drove down the boulevards. On the street corners, Nazi soldiers stood with their Gewehr 41 rifles hanging from their shoulders. The normal French center of an agricultural area had turned into a military fortress. Snow kept falling.

"There are so many," Herrick said. "So many troops."

"Ya." Arnwolf tapped a cigarette on his silver holder. "This city is the ideal route either to Pointe du Hourdel on the west coast or further north to Calais and the strait of Dover." Arnwolf lit the cigarette. "When the Allies try to land on the continent, their army will land somewhere in that stretch of coast. We are obviously ready for them." He raised an eyebrow. "Makes the perfect escape route for fleeing soldiers as well."

Herrick kept studying the street. "I hope we are well prepared."

"It will take them months to come," Mandel said. "By then, we will be even more entrenched. The Allies are doomed to failure. The world has never seen fighting troops like our German men."

"We said that when they marched into Russia," Herrick answered. "I don't think our efforts have been invincible in the east."

Mandel blew smoke out the window. "Don't worry. The Soviets will crumble in due time. A little setback here and there only delays the ultimate triumph."

Karl Herrick didn't answer.

"I'm sure that I'll get no information out of the army. Colonel Bern Schmidt suggested that local officers would be distant. I got the same suggestion from Berg Heydrich. He said that we have an agent here and that I should talk with him."

"Which way do you honestly think these Allied soldiers will flee?" Herrick asked.

"Pointe du Hourdel is closer to us, but farther from England," Mandel reasoned. "My hunch would be that they would take the longer route toward Calais which puts them much closer to the coasts of Dover. I'd bet on that path."

"Time is running out," Herrick observed. "If we don't catch them, they're gone forever."

"When we searched down the Sambre Meuse River, I was determined they would not elude me. Time has only sharpened my determination." Mandel stared out the car window. "We must not be slack."

At that moment an old truck lumbered into the square. Mandel could see a young boy driving with a huge man sitting next to him. The truck swung around the monument in the center of the park and chugged past their Mercedes. Three or four workers appeared to be huddled together sitting in the back end.

"Why would farm workers be out in this lousy weather?" Mandel asked.

"Maybe, they're doing road work or possibly attending cows," Herrick answered. "Farm fields and cattle are everywhere."

"Strange," Mandel mumbled, watching the truck turn away from the square taking the highway toward the northwest. "Where does that road go?"

"Up toward Doupliens and Burburn," Herrick said.

"And beyond that?"

"At the very end is Calais."

"*Calais!*" Mandel sat up in the seat.

"Don't worry. I'm sure the Americans would never venture close to the city of Amiens," Herrick said. "Too many soldiers around here to catch them." He pulled the car to a stop.

"I suppose so." Arnwolf Mandel opened the car door. "Let's go see the Gestapo agent in charge of this area."

Both men walked briskly into the office inside the court-house. Mandel flashed his papers and credentials. The staff immediately responded with respect.

"I need to make a phone call back to Paris," Mandel said. "Might I use your telephone?"

"But of course." The secretary offered the phone and walked away.

Arnwolf Mandel started dialing the hotel where he expected Arabella Kersten to be waiting by the phone. If she wasn't, there would be big trouble.

"Give me room 609," Mandel told the clerk at the desk.

"*Hallo,*" a woman's voice answered.

"Arabella?" Mandel snapped.

"Arnie! Where in the world are you?"

"I'm in the town of Amiens," Mandel said. "I was checking to see if you are okay."

"Oh, sure. Fine. Do you mind if I go out for a bit?"

Mandel thought for a moment. She'd been there like he told her. A good sign. Why not?

"I wouldn't be gone long but I did want to see the city some," Arabella cooed.

"Pay attention. Be careful."

"Where will you be tonight?" Arabella asked.

"Don't know. Probably somewhere up toward Calais."

Arabella giggled. "You be a good boy."

"I always am." Arnwolf Mandel hung up, feeling pleased with how this woman seemed to be staying with his exact directions. He liked obedience.

When Monique Sernin left Amiens, she did not drive the truck to the north but turned to the left, driving due west. By afternoon, she reached the town of Abbeville not far from Pointe du Hourdel near the ocean. The snow had quit falling, yet the temperature hadn't risen. Burnell Manville rightly reasoned that they would have to stop soon lest the Americans and the men in the back freeze.

Monique pulled the truck onto a side street in the old town and turned off the engine. Everyone piled out.

"What's happening?" Hank Holt asked.

"We need to talk a bit," Burnell said. "You boys gather around the truck to keep the wind from blowing on us. We're close enough to the ocean that the wind is colder."

"You ought to try the rear end of the truck," Jack Martin said. "Quite a charming winter ride back there."

Manville grinned. "I'm sure it is. Then again, it beats a German concentration camp."

"Not complaining," Jack said. "Just sharing information."

Monique looked up and down the street. "There aren't so many Germans here as there were in Amiens. They're around though. Don't make the mistake of thinking we're out of their control."

"She's right," Manville said. "Amiens was a juncture. That's why you saw so many trucks and soldiers. This town's not so significant."

"We're staying here tonight?" Hank asked.

"I think the weather is getting cold enough that we will have to," Manville said. "Trouble is, we don't know of any abandoned houses in the town. We didn't plan to stop here. It's possible to sleep in the back of the truck, but we've got to find some house or enclosed shed to get any real sleep. I don't like it. Not a good crack to fall in."

Gano Etienne nodded. "Don't like it at all."

"What's your best suggestion?" Jack asked the big man.

"I say we go to a café, a bistro, whatever we can find, and eat," Monique said. "The last couple of days have been on the lean side. After a good meal, we can start searching for a house. It's early enough we can eat before the Germans pile in."

"She's got a point," Hank said. "Get in and get out before Hitler shows up."

Manville nodded. "Let's go. I saw a restaurant around the corner." He looked critically at Monique. "Keep that cap pulled down over your face. Don't want them to see you're a woman."

The crew of six trudged a block to the café. Manville did most of the talking and soon bowls of hot soup were brought out from the kitchen. The waitress carried large loaves of bread and plates of steaming *beef le boeuf* with *le legumes*. A pitcher of steaming *café Parisian* was set out for the coffee drinkers. No one talked. Each person ate like it might be the last hot meal for days. When they had finished, Manville paid the waitress and they went back outside to their truck. The sun had begun to set and the winds were picking up again. Clearly they needed to do something about shelter for the night.

"Let's get back in the truck and drive around for a while," Jack suggested. "Maybe something will turn up."

"Yeah," Hank added. "That's a good idea."

Manville looked at Monique. She nodded and got back in the truck. They started down the street.

Jack quickly realized time was becoming a factor. They needed to come up with a room quickly or the night would swallow them. Monique turned a corner and saw a small hotel. She stopped. Manville got out and came around to the back.

"Let me see if I can rent one or two rooms and smuggle everyone in," the big man said. "We haven't seen another barn or other type of house."

"Is it safe?" Jack asked.

"That's the big question." Manville shook his head. "I must go in and see."

"What do you think?" Hank asked Jack quietly.

"We're going to freeze out here. I don't think we've got much option."

Hank nodded.

"I'll go with you, Burnell," Jack said. "Protect your back."

"Okay. Let's go."

The two men walked slowly across the street as if they were in no hurry. When they entered the hotel, an elderly woman was standing behind the worn counter with a worried look on her face. The ancient sitting room had bad lighting and dilapidated furniture. Jack saw two German soldiers standing against the back wall talking. His heart beat faster.

Manville nodded to the woman at the desk in a friendly manner and started speaking French. The woman didn't smile, but glanced toward the soldiers. Her eyes burned with a "watch out" message. Manville kept speaking in a low voice. Jack had no idea what they were saying, but the conversation seemed to have become detailed. The big man slipped some money over the counter.

"*Merci beaucoup*," the old woman said, her countenance returning to the glum frown.

Manville walked out with Jack following him.

"We've got a room," Manville said. "Most of us will have to sleep on the floor. There's not another hotel in town with room the woman told me. You saw the Krauts?"

Jack nodded. "Couldn't miss 'em."

"The old lady whispered to watch out for the soldiers. They check people."

Within a few minutes Burnell Manville had parked the truck on a side street. The six-member crew staggered their entry into the hotel. Over a period of thirty minutes, they crept up the wooden stairs and found the room on the second floor. When Jack and Hank came in, the German soldiers were still standing in the shadows watching people. Jack tried to climb the stairs without appearing to have leg injuries. After a couple of steps, he knew it was impossible and tried to swing his legs without looking like a cripple. The effort proved hopeless and finally he staggered off the top step in pain.

"You okay?" Hank asked.

"I'll live," Jack said. "Afraid stairs are my downfall."

"Let's get to the room." Hank started reading the numbers

on the doors. "Need to get you out of the hallway." He knocked lightly on the correct door and it opened. The two men hurried inside.

"You don't look so good," Monique told Jack.

"Stairs really stretch the skin on my legs." Jack eased down on the end of the bed. "I'm sorry, but I get in trouble every time I have to climb."

"Well, at least we're in out of the cold," Manville said. "Beats a night out there in that bitter wind."

The Etienne brothers nodded their heads.

"We've got one bed," Hank said. "I suppose the rest of us will sleep on the floor."

"We can put two people in the bed," Manville said. "I think burned legs need a mattress."

"No, no!" Jack objected. "I can sleep on the floor. No problem."

"No problem?" Manville grinned that impish smile. "I'd say you have more than little problem."

A sharp rap on the door stopped all conversation. Manville put his finger to his lips and tiptoed to the door. *"Oui?"*

A second hard knock followed. *"Offen!"*

Manville looked menacingly at each of his friends and finally shrugged. He unlocked the door and opened it slightly. The door flew open, hitting him in the chest and causing him to step back. The two German soldiers who had been standing downstairs pushed into the room.

"Aufmerksamkeit!" The German beckoned for the other soldier to follow him. They marched in, pointing at Jack Martin.

Jack looked up from the bed in horror. The Jerries were on to him.

The German pointed at his legs. *"Un hinken?"*

"Ya," Jack said.

The two soldiers looked at each with suspicion in their eyes.

"Ah!" The second soldier started taking his rifle off his shoulder. *"Un spitzel!"*

"Nein!" Jack protested.

The lead soldier stepped back and reached for his pistol. Hank suddenly leaped on the man yanking his hand away from the holster. The two men tumbled to the floor. Before the second man could release the safety on his rifle, Burnell Manville hit him so hard in the face that the German flattened over the bed. The Etienne brothers leaped into the fight. The German on the floor shouted, but Gano rammed his knife into the man's throat. The yell faded into a gargle of agony. Manville grabbed the only chair in the room and crashed it on the head of the soldier sprawled over the bed. No one moved.

"Th-they saw my legs," Jack sputtered. "Coming up the stairs. Th-thought I was on the run."

Gano Etienne pushed past Hank Holt and with one hard lunge stabbed the German on the bed through the heart.

"We're going to have to run," Monique said. "They'll miss these Nazis."

Manville nodded. "The old woman won't tell them anything. I think we need to find a back door though." He rubbed his chin for a moment. "Gano, go find a rear exit. We'll push these bodies under the bed and straighten up the room."

"Where will we go?" Gano asked.

"Into the night," Manville said. "Cold or not. We've got no choice left but to drive north toward Etaples. Grab the extra blankets."

Jack gritted his teeth. A freezing night. Another brush with death. The only good thing he could see was that they'd had a big supper. He pulled himself up from the bed and looked down. Only then did he look fully into the face of the man on the floor. This time the German certainly wasn't a boy. The man had hard, rugged features. Probably would have shot him without batting an eye.

Hank stood beside him, still staring at the body.

"You saved my life," Jack said and patted Hank on the back. "That's a second time. I owe you a big one."

Hank didn't smile.

CHAPTER TWENTY

Arabella Kersten stood in front of the mirror in the Paris hotel room brushing her long dark hair. Since childhood, she had followed her mother's persistent instructions to brush her hair one hundred strokes every day. *Mutter's* guidelines were always considered right and absolute. Following such simple but definite directives taught Arabella to be obedient even when she wanted to run in the opposite direction.

The Kersten family had been Lutherans for as many generations as anyone in her family had kept records, and they listened to the church. The teaching of the Lutheran church was that the gospel had come as the right hand of God's intervention in this world of sinful creatures. Believers who accepted the truth of faith would naturally do the right and loving deeds the gospel taught them. On the other hand, the law and courts represented God's left hand imposed on the disobedient for their trespasses. Rigid enforcement of the "narrow path" had supported a strict military mentality that ran through the German nation. One must do the right thing or face the consequences.

Doing the right thing was Arabella's problem. While gathering eggs in the barn at age thirteen, she had gotten into a wrestling match with her cousin Arne, a fifteen-year-old boy well on the road to becoming a young man. One thing led to another. Tumbling in the hay had turned into much more, and Arabella found she liked being with this cousin she'd always been attracted to. She knew these encounters were wrong, but Arabella certainly wasn't going to discuss her affair with anyone. After all, didn't the church promote experiences of love? Hard to say for certain. Naturally her mother would have come unglued. Arabella remained among the sinful creatures.

In those days everyone was struggling to survive the terrible depression that had destroyed the German economy. The value of the Deutschmark continually dropped and no one had time to watch the two cousins, so they sneaked off to the barn every chance they got. In time, the economy forced Arne and his family to move across Germany to a new town where they eventually became Nazis. Trips to the haystack were over, and fourteen-year-old Arabella was a child with the libido of a forty-year-old woman. She was caught in the middle of tension between being a consistent churchgoer in a Christian community promoting high values and, at the opposite end of the spectrum, having the disposition of a village floozy. While the tension proved to be a personal problem, it turned out to be quite helpful in her service to her political ideals.

Arabella fastened her shoes and looked in the mirror again. Arnwolf Mandel always liked gobs of makeup with heavy lipstick which she thought made her appear cheap. This morning she had done nothing more than wash her face, and that was all she was going to do. The plainness of her skin without any powdery covering pleased Arabella. No lipstick today. She was not in harness to any man and planned to keep it that way.

Slipping on her winter coat, Arabella locked the hotel door behind her and started down the hall that would take her to the streets of Paris. At the first subway station, she took the train to the usual stop for her clandestine meetings. As the car rumbled down the tracks, Arabella chuckled. Arnwolf Mandel would be shocked beyond belief should he learn she had come to Paris many times and had already visited art galleries, and certainly the Louvre. She was far more apt at picking up on his ineptitude than the Gestapo agent would have ever dreamed. The coach slid to an abrupt stop and Arabella Kersten got off.

Walking up cement steps, the woman found her way back onto a boulevard of Paris. Arabella spotted the metal bench where she always met her contact. For five minutes cars and buses drove down the busy street. Just as the street lights came on, a man wearing a brown trench coat and a red scarf came up from the subway. For a moment, Carlo Roche looked up and down the street before walking over and sitting down.

"Been here long?" the man asked.

"Long enough to survey the neighborhood," Arabella said. "I don't think we have any problems."

"Good." Carlo Roche pulled out a pack of cigarettes. "Want one?"

"Yes, but I better not. Makes us look too cozy."

Carlo Roche grinned. "You never miss a lick. Good thinking."

"That's why I'm still in business," Arabella said.

"What have you got for me?" Roche blew smoke into the air.

"You need to get a message to the boys. My Gestapo boyfriend is on his way to Calais. I think he's chasing cargo going north."

The agent look shocked. "Are you sure?"

"Just a few hours ago I talked to Mandel on the phone. He was in Amiens ready to go north."

The Comete Line agent nodded. "Arabella, you are the best secret we've got, but sometimes I wish your information came faster."

"I can convey only as fast as I get the news," Arabella said. "Hope you can make contact."

"That's the problem." Carlo Roche stood up. "Won't be easy. I'll have to get on the problem immediately."

"I'll let you know as soon as I hear more."

The Comete Line agent hurried back down the stairs to the subway.

Arabella stayed on the bench, watching the traffic. Being a spy wasn't easy, but the job gave her the opportunity to fight the Nazis she hated.

Night had fallen along the road from Abbeville running north toward Boulogne-sur Mer and Saint-Martin. The old truck bounced through the thick blackness along the highway until they came to the line dividing the province of Picardie from Nord-Pas de Calais. Drifting snow had tapered off, but the temperature continued to drop to an unusually low level for late November. The Etienne brothers huddled together with Jack Martin and Hank Holt to keep warm. Piled under the blankets they had taken from the hotel, as well as what they brought with them, the men struggled to keep from freezing.

Shortly after they crossed into the next province of Nord-Pas de Calais, a road sign pointed to the left and the ocean. The town of Berck wasn't far away and Burnell Manville had already fallen asleep. Monique slowed.

"Wake up, you old frog!" Monique demanded through the darkness.

"Huh!" The large man jerked straight up. "What? What's happened?"

"You fell asleep," Monique scolded. "With those brave men freezing in back, you drifted off in utter contentment. Shame on you!"

Manville folded his arms over his chest. "Humph!" he grumbled.

"We are at the turnoff to the town of Berck," Monique explained. "It's a ways before we hit another town. Should we take the road and see what turns up?"

"Why not?" Manville said. "Be best for our boys in back."

Monique slowed the truck and pulled off the main highway. The dirt road turned out to be filled with potholes. The dilapidated truck bumped up and down, slinging the men in back around like potatoes in a gunnysack. Monique was forced to drive slowly because of the poor condition of the road. Only one of the truck's headlights worked, and with each bump, the beam shot off at an odd angle, making it difficult to see the road well.

"Look!" Manville pointed toward the right. "Looks like a building up there!"

Monique slowed the truck. "I think it . . . it's . . . a school."

"Perfect. We can spend the night in that one-room school building. Let's get in there!"

"Don't get excited," Monique said. "Take it one step at a time."

"You're being difficult. Trying to irritate me?"

"Don't have to try," Monique said. "Comes naturally."

"You'll be sorry one of these day that you were so rude to me." Manville shook his finger at her.

"Don't push your luck," Monique said indifferently and pulled behind the school.

"Doesn't look like a large building." She turned off the engine. "Maybe no one uses the school now."

The men piled out of the back and hustled around the side of the truck. Blowing on their cold hands, no one said anything.

"We're back to taking what we can find," Manville said.

"Let's see if we can locate a door or window open. We need to get in out of the cold."

The men started trying every entry. Gano Etienne suddenly called around from the rear. By the time they had gotten around the building, Gano had climbed in an unlocked window and was hurrying through the building. His steps echoed into the dark night.

"He'll let us in the front door," Manville said. "Let's get inside." They followed him around to the front.

"Any lights in here?" Jack peered into the dark room.

"Doesn't look like the electric power's on," Monique said. "I've got some candles we had in the truck. I'll set them up and get some light going."

"The Nazis probably shut the electric power off in the entire area," Manville speculated. "We've got to have a story to tell if they come snooping around."

"Tell 'em we're farmers who got cut off from our sheep that we're still hunting," Jack suggested. "We're here because we can't find them."

"As good a story as any," Monique said. "We can say we're from Fort-Mahort. The town's close."

"There's likely to be more than two soldiers this time," Manville said, looking straight at Hank Holt. "I'd suggest we *not* try to jump them on this go round. Might prove to be nasty for us."

Hank grinned. "Strange how these things work out."

"Yeah," Manville growled, "and sometimes *don't* work out."

"Okay, okay, I'll try to be a tad more relaxed," Hank said.

"I can cook in the fireplace," Monique said. "Shouldn't put out too much light in the morning. The sooner we get to sleep the better."

Manville pointed around the room. "Grab a corner where you can keep warm. It's the best we can do."

Arnwolf Mandel and Karl Herrick had not gotten to Calais by nightfall. At the crossroads of the highway running from Longuenesse to Saint-Martin by the ocean they encountered a German military checkpoint. After presenting their credentials, Mandel engaged the commanding lieutenant in a discussion about their problem of catching the fleeing Allied soldiers. Herrick retired from the debate to call the Gestapo office in Paris for any new information that might have come in.

Mandel vehemently hated to admit he was wrong in any public discussion. Still, the evidence seemed to suggest that his original idea had been incorrect. Possibly the Allied lamsters hadn't run to the north, but taken a more circuitous route. He paced back and forth in the small room.

"Are you certain the Allies didn't slip past you?" Mandel pressed.

The *Wehrmacht* officer stiffened and began thumping his palm with a riding crop. "*Mein Herr,* you are trying to cover a large area. Why would you focus on one city on the coast as the logical town for them to hide in?"

"Because Calais is the port closest to England," Mandel snapped. "They've got to be in that area."

The officer raised an eyebrow. "We have told you all we can. I can assure the Gestapo that anyone traveling from Amiens to Calais would find it impossible to elude us."

Arnwolf Mandel rubbed his chin. "May I continue to study your maps?"

"Of course." The lieutenant turned on his heels and marched out of the tent.

Mandel stood by himself, feeling the condescending attitude of the officer. The *Wehrmacht* didn't like the Gestapo and didn't approve of secret police tactics. Probably this incompetent fool was sandbagging him. On the other hand, the man could be right.

Karl Herrick hurried into the tent. "*Mein Leiter!* An important report came in from Abbeville! The city due east from Amiens! Two of our soldiers were murdered in a hotel. Their bodies were found pushed under a bed."

"Abbeville?" Mandel picked up the detailed map. "Let me look."

"It's a longer route, but avoids major checkpoints like this one," Herrick explained. "If French insurgents were leading them, it would be a natural route up the coast."

"Hmm," Mandel studied the map. "Yes. Yes. If someone were guiding them with knowledge of these checkpoints, the path would fit."

"We don't get many of our men knifed and stuffed under hotel beds," Herrick observed. "Sounds like an altercation occurred in the hotel and the Allied escapees jumped our troops."

"Yes," Mandel said thoughtfully. "You're onto something. We should go due west to the town of Saint-Martin and Boulogne-sur-Mer instead of continuing on to Calais. Possibly we can head them off as they come up the coast."

Herrick clicked his heels and deferred with a nod of his head.

Arnwolf Mandel walked out of the tent and nodded to the lieutenant. *"Danken!"* He plunged his arm straight up in the air. *"Heil Hitler!"*

The lieutenant returned the salute but said nothing.

Mandel and Herrick drove off in the direction of Saint-Martin and the English Channel.

CHAPTER TWENTY-ONE

When the first light of morning streamed through the windows, the Comete Line crew began rolling out of their blankets. Jack struggled to stand up but couldn't. Sleeping on an unforgiving wooden floor had made his back as painfully stiff as his legs. He found it difficult to do much more than move to his side.

"Looks like you need a hand," Hank Holt observed.

"Afraid so." Jack rubbed his eyes. "How's your back?"

"About as pliable as a piece of oak wood." Hank forced himself to his feet. "Sleeping on a rock-hard floor will make an old man out of you." He stuck out his hand to help Jack up. "I'll pull you carefully, ole buddy."

Jack got hold of his friend's wrists and hung on. Hank carefully pulled him to his feet.

"It'll take me a while to get moving," Jack said. "Let me stretch. I'll get my muscles working eventually."

The rest of the crew seemed to move slowly this morning as well. The Etienne brothers picked up the blankets, folded them, and put the woolen covers in the back of the truck. Monique stirred the fire that Burnell Manville had built. With the remnants of the sausage they brought from Paris and a loaf of bread, she laid out a meager breakfast that could be quickly consumed. No one said much as they each silently ate, thinking about their own individual worries and concerns.

"What day is it?" Jack abruptly asked.

Manville looked at Monique and shrugged. "I don't know. Do you?"

"November 25," Monique said. "Why?"

"It's Thanksgiving Day!" Jack exploded. "Hey, it's our national day to thank God for His blessings!"

"What?" Manville frowned. "Never heard of it."

"In America our families gather on this day to thank God for the bountiful harvest," Jack explained. "It's a good time to rejoice in the goodness of our God as well as feast with our families."

Gano Etienne shook his head and uncharacteristically spoke. "What's God got to do with eating well? With anything?"

"Anything?" Jack recoiled. "He's the source of *everything*."

"Like this meager breakfast this morning?" Gano grinned cynically. "A few hunks of fat ground up with pig and served with a glass of water?"

"Better than nothing," Jack retorted. "At least, we had a roof over our heads last night and something to eat this morning. I'm grateful."

Gano shrugged. "We don't keep this festival in France."

"Don't mind him," Monique said. "Gano is always a pessimist. He's our soldier philosopher. Listens to people like Albert Camus. Doesn't believe in anything and hates the church." She turned back to Jack. "Tell us about this festival."

"We commemorate the survival of the pilgrims who founded our country," Jack explained. "After a cold, hard winter they realized that the goodness of God had kept them alive through the hardest of days. Thanksgiving reminds us of our dependency on our Creator. On Thanksgiving Day we remember that our heavenly Father is the source of the capacity to endure in the worst of times."

"But couldn't this God of yours have kept you out of the 'worst of times,' as you call this day?" Gano argued.

"Tough times make tough people," Hank Holt added. "We don't have to fear the trials that test us."

"You are a rationalist," Gano countered, "and I think you are also a sentimentalist who uses the idea of God like a bandage to cover wounds that the world inevitability imposes on everyone."

"And I think you are an atheist who attempts to destroy people's convictions," Monique argued. "A bitter cynic. You'd do well to listen to this American."

Gano shrugged again and looked away.

"Here's to everyone!" Jack held up his cup of water. "Even in these difficult times, we toast each other and wish everyone the best. Thanks be to God!"

"Hear! Hear!" echoed around the room.

Jack went back to eating the greasy piece of sausage lying in front of him. Gano had been right. There wasn't much on the table. No turkey, dressing, or cranberry fluff this year. A few slices of old sausage weren't much to exchange for sweet potatoes and pecan pie, but that was the wrong measuring stick. He wasn't sitting in a concentration camp where he might starve to death. Sure, he'd been cold, but that didn't keep the warm sun from rising on a new day. Even with his injuries, he had survived an impossible chase across two countries. The pain in his legs reminded Jack that he was still alive—and that was no small accomplishment. Yes, the days had been hard. Nevertheless, it was ultimately the hand of God that had provided the antibiotics and the doctor in the Brusselmans' house. Of course, Julien and Ann Brusselman and their children had been a pure gift during those tense days. Even though it was small, the sausage was a reminder that God remained with them.

At that moment, a new idea popped into Jack's mind. The capacity to have gratitude was shaped by which end of the measuring stick one used. He must remember what is at hand, not what he might have had at some other place and time. Deprivation, not abundance, imparts the truest perspective. The hand of God had provided, and that was all that counted.

Jack finished eating the last piece of sausage and took a swig of water. He was alive. That was enough for a Thanksgiving.

The flames in the old schoolhouse's fireplace had been snuffed out and the room put back in order like the Comete Line crew had found it. Anyone with an attentive eye could spot the marks on the floor, but overall, the building didn't appear used. Each piece of furniture was carefully put back in place. The crew needed to get on their way and leave a secured building behind them.

"Everyone load up," Burnell Manville shouted. "We need to get a move on."

Jack Martin backed onto the rear end of the truck and pushed himself forward toward the cab. Hank helped pull him along. The Etienne brothers piled in and Monique turned on the engine, letting it run to warm up. During the night, snow had drifted in from the fields and little piles lay around the yard. She raced the engine several times to make sure the motor functioned.

"Uh, oh!" Jack pointed toward the road. "Don't look now, but there's a truckload of Germans coming our way."

Hank sheltered his eyes from the sun. "Lord, help us! There's no way we can even get around them. We're trapped!"

The military truck lumbered slowly up the road. Jack could see eight Germans in the back with rifles on their shoulders while two men sat in the front seat. Their truck didn't seem to be coming at a fast pace as if they were prepared to attack. From the looks of things, it was more of an inspection. Monique turned the truck around. When she faced the Nazis, Monique stopped, probably seeing the Germans for the first time. Jack had to look through the back window to see what was going on. Off in the distance he heard the sound of airplane engines roaring toward them.

What a mess to be in! The Nazis were in front of them, and who knew what might be coming down out of the sky? Jack clenched the side of the truck bed. He had no idea what was heading their way, but nothing felt right. He could see the airplane turning, preparing for a swoop down on them. At that moment he recognized the familiar shape of two Curtis P-40 *Flying Tiger* fighters turning toward them.

"They're our boys!" Jack told Hank. "They're on our side!"

"Yeah, but they don't know that!" Hank started inching down against the back of the cab. "They may come after us."

"*Halten!*" one of the German soldiers shouted as the truck came to a stop.

Monique slammed on the brakes.

Another German pointed to the sky and started yelling.

The P-40s roared out of the sky with their machine gun fire roaring. They were clearly aiming at the troop carrier but the ammunition flew in every direction. Jack heard the sound of metal ripping and glass scattering around him. The Etienne brothers jumped up and ran to get out of the truck. A third P-40 came out of nowhere, spraying bullets behind the path of the first two airplanes. Their truck rocked as bullets flew through the cab. Jack flattened against the truck bed and tried to cover his head.

The Germans' military carrier roared to life and whirled around in front of them, dashing in the opposite direction back toward the road. When the Nazis hit the corner where the school road met the highway, one of the Curtis P-40s had returned and opened fire on the German truck. Jack saw the vehicle swerve back and forth before it flew off the road and exploded.

The entire episode had taken virtually no more than a minute, but it seemed like an eternity. Jack pushed himself up to assess what had happened to them. He saw that Monique had dived out of the cab and was lying on the ground beside the truck.

"Monique! You hurt?" Jack yelled.

"No," she said feebly. "Just got the wind knocked out of me."

"They aren't okay," Hank said from the end of the truck. He pointed at Eliot and Gano Etienne sprawled on the ground. "Both hit with the heavy machine gun fire."

"No!" Jack groaned. "No." The brothers lay side by side on their faces. "Not our guys!"

Monique pushed herself up from the ground. "We've got to get out of here!" she yelled. "No telling what's happening next."

"Manville," Jack called out. "What do we do?"

No answer.

"Where'd he go?" Jack slid out of the back of the truck.

"A-w-w-!" Monique shrieked and crumpled.

Jack ran around to the side of the truck where Monique had opened the door. Burnell Manville lay hunched over the dashboard with his head lying outside the windshield that had been blown out. Two machine gun bullets had ripped through the big man's chest.

"O-o-o-h!" Jack staggered away from the truck. "Manville's dead!"

Hank started to enter the cab and then drew back. "He's gone," Hank mumbled. "We're helpless."

Jack leaned against the truck to keep from heaving. "Our friend is dead!" He put his hands to his face. "They've killed our people."

Monique held onto the truck door for a moment, trying to regain her composure. She slowly straightened. Suddenly Monique grabbed Jack by the shirt and shook him. "Stop it!" she demanded. "We've got to get out of here."

"What do we do?" Hank asked.

"Leave the truck!" Monique ordered. "We've got to make it look like everyone got killed. You've got no choice but to walk across that snow-covered field." She pointed north and toward the highway. "I don't care how bad your legs hurt. Grab those crutches and run."

Jack pulled out the tree limbs Monique had whittled into crutches for him days earlier.

"Listen to me," Monique warned. "We can't afford any mistakes. The highway's not too far away. We've got to get there. It's not much of a hope but it's the only one we've got. If you boys believe in prayer, you better start praying. Now move it!"

The harsh winter wind had settled and snow no longer fell, but walking through the icy field proved to be as painful as

Jack had imagined. Rough, frozen dirt clods kept tripping him. Cold temperatures made his burned skin tight and only caused the journey to be more difficult. Fighter aircraft kept buzzing the terrain and added to the tension. After an hour Jack, Hank, and Monique reached the highway that ran north to Saint-Martin and stopped by a fence constructed from piled rock.

"You making it?" Monique quipped.

"Have to," Jack answered and leaned on the crutches.

"I imagine your feet are killing you," Hank added.

"Slightly," Jack said. "A bit cold. Like two icebergs."

Monique nodded, acknowledging the problem but giving no sympathy. "We've got no choice. We have to keep going. Maybe nobody will find our truck; maybe they will discover the bodies quickly enough. Just can't tell."

"What will the Germans figure?" Jack asked.

"They might think that airplanes strafed them," Monique said thoughtfully. "On the other hand, they could decide that our boys ambushed the soldiers. In that case, they'd conclude there was a shootout that killed everyone."

"What about us?" Hank asked. "Will they notice our escape?"

"Let's hope not," Monique said. "That's why we've got to keep moving."

"Walking won't cut it," Jack said. "Not fast enough. You may have to leave me behind and pick up the pace."

"You're the reason we're making the mad dash for the ocean," Monique said. "Cut out that kind of talk." She shaded her eyes and looked up and down the road. "We're going to try to catch a ride on the back of a farm truck. I think that's the best way."

"What about a train?" Jack asked.

"We might have to grab one, but it's certainly not the safest way," Monique said. "First, your legs prohibit fast movement. Trains fly along. Second, the Nazis pay close attention to the trains. We'd probably be overextended, especially this close to the ocean." She pointed to the north. "Let's keep walking."

Jack hobbled along on the pavement. Walking was easier on the asphalt topping, but the cold kept his feet numb and his shins ached. Gritting his teeth, he forced himself to keep moving while every nerve in his body rebelled. Jack kept swinging his wooden crutches forward as they steadily walked the highway to the north.

In another thirty minutes, Jack was sure that his burned skin was at the point of cracking and bleeding if it already wasn't. Maybe it had already, but he knew better than to mention the problem. They had to keep moving and all he'd be was a drag. The crutches dug into his armpits and rubbed against his chest. If he stopped, their cause was lost. If he kept walking, eventually he would collapse. Jack lost either way. The only alternative was to grit his teeth and keep hobbling to the end.

"Look!" Monique pointed behind them. "A farmer's coming up the road. See! He's riding on a horse-drawn wagon."

Jack slumped on his crutches and caught his breath. Silently, he prayed for relief. Sitting in an old wagon would do just fine.

Monique started waving frantically. An old man with a cloth tied around his head to keep his ears warm sat behind a horse pulling the wagon. With a white beard, the farmer looked on the ancient side. The back of his buckboard was piled high with a load of hay. The old man waved back.

"The elderly always hate the Germans," Monique said softly. "He's got to be one of us. Let's find out."

Still waving, the young woman walked up to the wagon. French rolled out so fast that Jack had no clue what she was saying. He stood waiting, praying for a kind heart in the old man.

Monique grinned and patted the man on the arm. Without returning to English, she gestured for the pilots to climb on the back. Jack and Hank settled into the loose hay, pulling the sheaves around them. The long strands proved to be an insulation from the cold and the wind. The wagon rolled on up the highway at a leisurely pace. Jack could hear Monique and the farmer talking but still couldn't make out a word. Curling up into a ball to keep warm, he pulled the hay over him, disappearing into the thick pile.

Thank God! Jack thought. *Anything is better than trudging through a frozen plowed field. Lord, please keep that horse moving.*

CHAPTER TWENTY-TWO

On the day that Gestapo agent Arnwolf Mandel arrived in Saint-Martin, he spent ten hours surveying the town and the road system that ran in and out of the French village. The next day the winds had settled and the snow stopped. Arnwolf pulled up the collar of his leather overcoat to protect his neck and walked out into the street once again. He was certain the Allied escapees would have to enter the town from the south. The issue was whether they would take the main road or try to circumvent the town by winding through the country roads. Because they had no idea anyone was chasing them, Arnwolf concluded they'd probably attempt to come through town confident they would face no more than the usual German checkpoint.

Mandel walked down the cobblestone street and watched the traffic rumble through the streets for a few minutes. Cars, men riding horses, and trucks lumbered through the town. He reasoned that the Americans would be disguised and probably attempt to look like Frenchmen. The problem was that the French looked many different ways: businessmen, merchants, farm workers, street cleaners, bakers, on and on. The last time he'd seen these men they were floating out of the sky on the end of parachutes. These Allied dogs had disappeared into the bushes without leaving clues. Of course, he knew one man was probably on crutches or limping, and that was an important problem that couldn't be hidden.

Arnwolf stopped and watched a German soldier directing traffic in the center of the town square. Each vehicle did exactly as the soldier directed them to do. No one dared get out of line or they'd pay a high price. The *Reich* had the town, the province, the country under firm control. Finding these fleeing prisoners shouldn't prove difficult.

Unfortunately, it was.

Arnwolf started back up the street. The *Wehrmacht* had been responsive when he explained his purpose in working in the Pas de Calais area. The army remained equally concerned to stop anyone from escaping, especially by crossing the English Channel. Any area vulnerable to the landing of the Allied Expeditionary Forces had to be protected with the utmost care and no one wanted to be accused of being slack. Letting two fleeing invaders get away would be a black mark. Arnwolf knew he could count on these troops at the checkpoints to support his effort.

Across the street, Arnwolf spotted a café. Perhaps, a coffee with a shot of brandy would warm him. Without waiting, Arnwolf cut across the street, paying no attention to who was coming. He walked in and sat down at one of the tables. No one talked in more than a whisper. Several men glanced at him with hostility in their eyes. Obviously, they knew he was either a stranger or a German agent. Intimidation pleased him. He smiled. Arnwolf enjoyed discouragement, and the German presence certainly imparted apprehension.

The Gestapo agent had nearly finished his coffee when the front door opened and Karl Herrick hurried in. Herrick had that usual panicked look on his face.

"Sit down, Karl. We have the situation in this town under control."

Herrick pulled off his hat and scooted up to the table. "I have been surveying the field reports all day. A few minutes ago an important communique came in from an old school near the town of Berck toward the south."

"Oh?" Arnwolf raised an eyebrow. "So?"

"One of our troop carriers ended up in the ditch with all the men but one found dead. Even though the one who survived was injured, he witnessed the entire scene. Our soldiers spotted a truckload of farmers leaving an abandoned schoolhouse and went to investigate when a squadron of fighter planes attacked and shot up both our men and the people trying to leave the schoolhouse. After the bodies were examined our agents think the farmers were actually underground saboteurs."

"Excellent!" Arnwolf's casual demeanor vanished. "Did they get our Allied escapees?"

Herrick shook his head. "No. The lone survivor saw two men and a woman escape into the fields."

"Two men and a woman!" Arnwolf pounded the table. "Now we know *exactly* what we are looking for."

"One of the men was using crutches."

"That's them!" Arnwolf stood up. "We need to be out there on the streets."

People around the café stopped talking and looked at him, obviously listening to Arnwolf.

He sat down quickly. "The question is when they will come this way."

"Hard to say," Herrick said. "They were last seen walking into the snow. Of course, they might catch a ride . . . a train . . . a farm truck . . . other underground associates. Difficult to predict."

"I am sure they must be traveling to some landing between here and Calais," Arnwolf thought out loud. "A small boat at least will be required to pick them up. In the meantime we must watch for two men and a woman."

"What is your plan, *mein leiter?*" Herrick fell back into his obedient voice.

"I'm not sure yet." Arnwolf stood up again. "Let us go outside and think about this problem further."

The two men walked back out into the cold street and strolled to the south. A large wagonload of hay came lumbering up the street with an old man driving. A young woman sat next to him. Mandel and Herrick kept walking and talking. The wagon disappeared down the street.

"Yes," Karl Herrick finally said. "I agree we must watch this road south toward Berck very carefully, but we must cover the north as well." He cleared his throat and spoke with a tentativeness about what he proposed. "Would it be of help if I stayed in the town of Saint-Martin while you went to Calais? Perhaps, we could form a sort of pincer approach. At least both ends of the spectrum would be covered."

Arnwolf walked half a block before he spoke. "If you were on one end and I on the other, we would have the advantage of squeezing these slithering snakes. We could pursue them from both ends."

"It would seem so," Herrick said slowly. "In Calais we also have an agent with an office at number 45 on Neuilly Street."

"You stay here!" Arnwolf demanded. "I will leave immediately for Calais and wait in that city. Yes, this is the perfect plan."

"You have an excellent idea," Herrick said.

"*Heil* Hitler!" Arnwolf shot his arm up in the air and hurried off in the direction of the car.

An unexpected temperature increase sent a warmer breeze into the town of Saint-Martin. The old man seated behind the horse flipped the reins to keep his steed walking briskly. The gelding pulling the truckload of hay plodded through the center of town and kept trudging onward. At the end of town, the farmer left the main highway and turned down a side road, veering toward the ocean. His persistent horse didn't slow, but kept trudging through the frozen mud.

When they reached the end of the lane, the farmer turned into a barnyard. Chickens and ducks flapped their wings and squawked but leaped out of his way. Without hesitating, the old man drove his wagon into the barn. Once inside he jumped off the wagon and hurried back to shut the barn doors. The young woman sitting next to him climbed down from the wagon seat.

"You can come out now," Monique shouted at the hay.

"Okay," a man's voice said from underneath the pile of straw. "We're tunneling out."

Once the old man shut the barn doors, he dropped a wooden plank into the spaces that secured the doors. He dusted off his hands and watched the two Americans climb out of the hay.

"Our friend speaks no English or German," Monique explained as the two Americans scooted out and climbed off the back of the buckboard. "He understands you don't speak French, but knows who we are. He's glad to help. I trust him. His name is Talon."

The old man nodded to the soldiers and smiled.

"He's going to help us by preparing a hot meal and will hide us until we are ready to leave," Monique said. "We're fortunate he picked us up."

Jack grinned and extended his hand. "Thank you, sir. *Merci beaucoup.*"

Talon kept grinning and shook hands. The farmer bobbed up and down as if he were bowing to royalty. He turned to Monique and told her in French that he liked the looks of these boys. He'd be back with food as quickly as possible. Turning toward a side door, the old man hustled away.

"This man is trustworthy," Monique explained. "We talked a long time before I explained who we were."

"You don't think he'll turn us in?" Hank pressed.

"No." Monique shook her head. "I am satisfied."

"Well," Jack said thoughtfully, "we have no alternative but to trust good ole Talon. At least this barn is warm."

"Yeah," Hank added. "Beats hoofing it down that frozen highway."

"I keep thinking about Burnell and the Etienne brothers," Jack said. "They died so quickly, so instantly. One minute we were talking and suddenly they were gone. I don't know . . . I guess . . . it leaves me feeling—"

"Stop it!" Monique said harshly. "We cannot afford to allow ourselves to discuss these incidents. If you do, emotion will swallow you alive. Yes, they were our friends, our comrades . . ." Monique's voice cracked and she stopped, pressing her hand to her mouth. "Our friends," she finally said. "But we must go on. Now stop talking about them." Monique turned away and walked to the other side of the barn.

For a long time no one said anything. Silence seemed more appropriate than talking. Each person found a different corner of the barn and acted like he was doing something when they did nothing. The loss had enveloped them. Eventually the barn's side door opened and the old man returned with food. Saying little, Talon spread a table for them. The threesome sat quietly and ate rapidly. The hot tea that the farmer brought was consumed until the pot was empty.

"I suppose the time has come to tell you the full truth," Monique broke the silence. "As Burnell said earlier, we keep information hidden lest someone is captured, but we are coming close enough to our destination that you should know all the facts. If the old man is able to find us a ride, we are close to the town of Calais. In that town the Comete Line has a special house where we hide Allied troops until we can put them in a boat for crossing of the English Channel. If anything happens to any of us, the others are to get to this house. Walk all the way, hobbling if necessary. Once you arrive, they will already know who you are and will start your final exit from France. Is that understood?"

Jack looked at Hank and nodded. "Got ya."

"Assume nothing," Monique said. "The Nazis are everywhere and the last leg of this journey is the most dangerous. When you reach Calais, you must go to the wharf along the ocean. You will find a street named St. Pierre that runs along the water. In the middle of this street is a house marked with a number 8. No matter what happens you must not approach this house until after nightfall. If a red scarf is hanging next to the front door, you can knock. If not, you must keep walking. Understood?"

Jack and Hank nodded.

"Won't you be with us?" Hank asked the French woman.

"I can't say. Maybe I will. We are at a point in this journey where nothing is predictable."

"Never thought it was," Hank said.

Silence settled over the group again. Each person ate thoughtfully and drank the hot tea without speaking.

"Do you ever pray?" Jack broke the silence.

Monique looked startled. "Pray? I pray nearly every second of this expedition. I virtually never stop."

Jack nodded. He knew Madame Brusselman prayed. She had certainly prayed for his health. Ann had been a woman of quiet dignity who went about her business of saving Allied soldiers without much being said about anything spiritual. The truth had been clear. She was devout. Monique was somewhat like Ann, but much more rough cut. No housewife for sure, Monique found sitting next to a farmer behind a horse far more her style. She could drive into the turf and come up spitting out the dirt without blinking an eye. Underneath the facade, Monique did pray. Perhaps, with the fervor of a soldier walking into the fire of an enemy squad of assassins. How unexpected that the Comete Line ran through the lives of so many different people who still depended on God to take them through the dark night.

Would they all make it? Reverend Harold Assink and the Brusselmans had; Burnell Manville, the Etienne brothers, Madame Somerville and Dirk Vogel hadn't. Maybe they wouldn't.

Jack didn't want to know, but he understood how important it was to pray. He would keep on asking God to lead them through this death trap no matter what happened. The journey took more than Hennie Matthys's brand of endurance. It took faith.

Flying down the highway to Calais, Arnwolf Mandel thought about Arabella Kersten and what she was doing at that moment. He hadn't called her and should have. Then again, the woman was little more than a toy. She'd stay put until he called with further instructions. Arabella had proved capable of following his instructions to the letter and that was what counted. After he caught those fleeing lamsters then he'd return to Paris and the good times could start again.

Arnwolf knew Germany stood on the edge of prosperity for all loyal citizens. Soon this war would be concluded and the resources of half of Europe would flow into the coffers of the Third Reich. In such a time of abundance, he would lavish in wealth as would other Germans who had been faithful to their *Führer*. Perhaps the Allies would come to their senses and sue for peace even before an invasion of Europe occurred. Certainly they would be much more intelligent to do so and save themselves the terrible ordeal that the *Wehrmacht* would deal out if they tried to come ashore. Whatever. Arnwolf gloried in being a Nazi, a part of the Aryan race that would dominate world history for a thousand years.

When the outskirts of Calais came into view, Arnwolf was surprised that the town was smaller than he imagined. He could catch occasional glimpses of the Strait of Dover and the ocean waves out beyond the beaches. The scene looked peaceful and quiet like most fishing villages, but Arnwolf knew the veneer remained only a facade. Underneath the appearances, both the Allies and the Axis were hard at work to defeat each other. He hoped the Gestapo agent in Calais was up on every detail of the current struggle. Arnwolf needed the man to be agile and adaptable. Hopefully, the local agent would prove to be easy to work with. Within the village of Calais had to be the payoff in his long struggle to catch the fleeing Allied pilots.

Wheeling past small stores, a bakery, shops, and a hotel, Arnwolf found his way to Neuilly Street where Herrick said the location of the Gestapo office would be. In the middle of the block, number 45 stood with no sign over the door. Arnwolf pulled up and went in. He had barely entered when a jovial little man rushed toward him with his arms extended.

"Ah! You must be *Herr* Mandel," he said. "I'm Gerhard Hackett. Your assistant Karl Herrick phoned you were coming." Hackett extended his hand. "Welcome to our offices."

Arnwolf Mandel shook hands and gave the *Heil Hitler* salute. The enthusiastic reception was more than he had expected.

"I understand you are about to apprehend two enemy scoundrels," Hackett continued. "Is it true that they are coming here?"

"I think so," Arnwolf said. "Every indication is that they are almost on your doorstep. The problem is finally locating them for arrest."

"I see," Gerhard Hackett said thoughtfully. "You don't know where they will land."

"Exactly."

Gerhard smiled. "Perhaps, we can be of significant assistance in this problem." He pulled out a cigarette case from his inner pocket and opened the metal tray. "Care for a cigarette?"

"Thank you." Arnwolf took out a cigarette and tapped it on the desk. Gerhard offered a light and the two men blew smoke into the air. "Excellent tobacco. Good quality."

"Of course." Hackett grinned. "Doesn't the Gestapo desire the best?"

Both men chuckled.

"I believe two men and a woman are on their way here to Calais," Arnwolf said. "I have every reason to believe that one of the men is on crutches or has a serious limp. In a town this size three strangers of that description shouldn't be that difficult to identify."

Gerhard Hackett nodded his agreement. "Two men and a woman. Hmm. Yes. Of course, they might disguise the woman, but a limp can't be covered."

"Do you have a suggestion where they might hide?"

Hackett smiled knowingly. "Of course! With the Reich's expectation that the Allies might attempt to land in this area, we scrutinize everything and everybody." He tapped his cigarette in the ashtray. "No, I haven't seen two men and a woman yet, but I have been watching a particular house where we believe the underground sends our enemies trying to escape from the country. For some time we've been observing this residence and have seen many suspects come and go."

"Excellent! Do you have an address?"

"Yes," Gerhard Hackett said. "It's on St. Pierre Street. Number 8."

CHAPTER TWENTY-THREE

No other alternative existed except to hide in Talon's barn. December was only around the corner but the weather became significantly warmer. Still, they slept under thick blankets. Months earlier a five-foot-deep hole had been dug under the dirt floor where as many as six people could hibernate at night. A wooden covering with empty cans attached to the wooden door hid the entryway and concealed the hidden space, allowing them to sleep in relative peace. Monique distanced herself and throughout the day kept pacing along the far wall alone.

The old farmer had turned out to be much more than a good friend. While not a participant, Talon knew about the Underground and was available to help in any possible way. He fussed over his guests and took a particular interest in the Americans. Talon had not figured out how to get them to Calais yet, but the old man was obviously working hard at coming up with something. Even though he had never owned a vehicle in his life and only had a rudimentary knowledge of how to drive one, Talon kept promising Monique that a bucket of bolts would turn up.

In the late afternoon Hank sat down next to Jack on an ancient wooden bench shoved next to the wall. Rays of sunlight pierced through the cracks in the worn boards, throwing long shadows across the straw-covered dirt floor. The sun's warmth felt encouraging.

"We've come a long way since we got blown out of the sky over Maastrich," Hank said. "I don't think you thought we'd survive our little swim down the Sambre Meuse River."

Jack chuckled. "You're right. Strange how that cold water cooled off my burns. The last person in the world that I'd expect to pull us out of the river was Dirk Vogel. A fine young man."

Hank nodded. "Hard to grasp that they killed him."

"I've almost turned clinically paranoid," Jack said. "Used to think the best of everybody. Now I doubt anyone I see."

"Only way to stay alive. We're dead men if we make one mistake."

"I keep seeing Burnell Manville stretched through that windshield," Jack said. "The sight paralyzes me. Makes me want to curl up in a ball and disappear."

"Yeah." Hank nodded his head. "Fear has become our new companion. We shake hands every morning and night."

"I'm tired of the routine. Be glad to pass on the greeting to someone else for a change."

"What will you do when we get back?" Hank asked.

"Do you think we will?"

"Sure." Hank grinned and then the smile slowly faded. "Honestly, I don't know. Can't let myself think about it. I know the odds are stacked against us. Even if we get to Calais without any more trouble, we've got to cross the ocean in cold weather with high, rugged waves. See what I mean?"

Jack nodded.

"You realize we'd never have gotten this far without all those good people helping us. Wonder what made them stick their necks out so far."

"Yeah, people like the Brusselmans and the Comete Line underground crawled out there with us to the absolute end of the branch. I guess they understand the Nazis even better than we do. Most people back in America don't understand what they should know for a fact. Freedom from tyranny can cost your life. We sit around in our malt shops and eat hamburgers like it's a God-given right. The truth is that liberty is an extremely expensive privilege. It may well cost us our lives before it's all over."

Hank swallowed hard and didn't say anymore.

By the time the sun had gone down, Monique had lit the candle that Talon brought out of the house earlier in the day. She kept it on the ground behind a wooden stall to minimize any light shining out of the barn. Most of the time Jack and Hank walked around in the darkness and took turns watching through the cracks between the boards on the side of the barn. A German patrol could turn up unexpectedly and they had to be prepared to jump in their sleeping hole if the Krauts came rolling down the road.

At nine o'clock Hank came back from his turn at looking out through the boards into the night and sat down next to Jack and Monique. "Know it's early, but I'm ready to get a long night's sleep. If we get into the town of Calais, tomorrow may prove to be a difficult day. Think I'll turn in."

"Ah, the darkness is just getting to you," Jack groused. "You're getting fidgety and turning into an old man like our buddy Talon. Wearing out, Hank?"

"Come the morning, you'll wish you'd turned in early." Hank stood up and started walking toward the dugout. "See you later."

"Just getting soft," Jack quipped.

Hank disappeared into the ground and let the wooden covering settle over him. Jack stuck his legs out to stretch the skin on his shins. Monique sat next to him watching the candle burn. With her legs pulled up under her chin, she sat with her head resting on her arms spread across her knees.

"You have a girl back home?" Monique asked.

"No," Jack said. "I was only eighteen when I got into this war. That was two years ago. Oh, I went out with a couple of high school friends. Nothing serious."

"Oh!" Monique smiled. "Interesting."

"You got a boyfriend?"

Monique stiffened. "I am older than you," she said. "Yes. Yes, I have had someone special to me."

"Where is he?"

Monique's jaw tightened. "He is gone."

"A soldier?"

"Of sorts."

"Off fighting on the war front?"

She shook her head. "No."

"Well, where's the guy today?"

Monique kept staring into the flame in the candle without speaking. Finally, she took a deep breath. "He's dead."

Jack caught his breath. "Oh no. Oh, I'm so sorry. When did this happen?"

"Three days ago."

Jack jerked and looked at the young woman incomprehensibly. "I-I d-don't think I understand."

Tears welled up in Monique's eyes. She dropped her head low and her body shook as she wept silently. "I-I told you that emotion can swallow you." Tears ran down her face. "You can't let yourself go to these hard places. It simply hurts too much."

"But . . . but . . . how did you find out he was killed?"

"Burnell Manville and I were lovers," Monique said. "We kept our relationship quiet, but I loved him deeply."

Jack put his arm around her and gave Monique a squeeze. "I'm so, so sorry. I had no idea."

Monique sobbed against Jack's shoulder until there seemed to be no more tears left. For a long time they sat quietly. Finally Monique dried her eyes.

"I haven't cried until now," Monique said. "I was afraid to break down back when I saw Burnell at the truck. I wanted to die, but I made myself move. We both recognized that we could be killed at any time. We had talked of it often, but no one is prepared when the moment comes. I knew we had to keep running or the Nazis would catch us."

"Yeah, I'm sure that was right." Jack pulled away from her. "Monique? How in the world did you ever get into working with such terrifying and deadly circumstances?"

Monique stared off into the blackness. The agonized expression did not leave her face. She didn't say anything for a long time. Jack waited silently.

"The Nazis attacked France in May of 1940," Monique said softly. "By June 14, the Germans had marched into Paris, sending millions of people fleeing the city. My family lived in the Parisian suburb of Gagny. We soon learned that all Jewish people had their French identity cards confiscated and were forced to wear yellow stars. Soon the SS started rounding up the Jews. The rumors were everywhere that they were being hauled off. My father went out to protest this inhumane activity." Monique's neck stiffened and her eyes became resolute. "The Nazis shot him. Stood my father against a wall in the street and killed him. I guess something died inside of me that day. That's when I decided to work for the Underground."

Jack didn't say anything more. Eventually the candle burned down to a nub. "I think we should crawl in the hole before all the light is gone," he said. "Are you ready?"

Monique nodded.

Without anything more being said, they prepared for the night.

A sputtering sound shook Jack Martin and forced him awake. In the darkness of their sleeping hole under the barn, noise of Germans at the door petrified Jack. Monique stirred. Hank grabbed her mouth to prevent any sound. As silent as granite rocks, each feared Nazi soldiers were about to capture them.

The wooden covering flew open and a face looked down.

"We leave!" Talon barked in broken English. "Time going."

"W-what?" Jack sat up. "Talon?"

"Have truck," Talon said. "*Oui!* Drive to Calais. Come. Breakfast."

The shaken friends climbed out of the hole. The wide open barn door revealed the source of Talon's pleasure. A rickety old Renault truck sat outside the door puttering laboriously. The big box-shaped cab with spoke-wheeled tires looked like it had been around for far more than several decades. From the rattling of the sputtering motor, the truck looked like it might not make it to Calais.

"You sure this rig works?" Hank scratched his head. "Doesn't sound exactly on the dependable side."

Monique put the question to Talon in French. The old man became animated.

"He insists it will," Monique said. "Let's not try his patience."

"*Merci beaucoup*," Jack said and shook the old man's hand. Talon beamed.

"I told you a long night's sleep would be needed," Hank said under his breath. "You're about to find out how big a difference it can make."

Jack grinned. "Come on. Be sporting, old man."

"We ain't playing football," Hank grumbled.

Breakfast was consumed without much being said until the eggs were gone. Monique leaned forward and spoke softly. "I am sure this truck will not go very fast, but the distance isn't great. Talon wants to put the two of you in back and cover you with sacks of feed. I don't think that is a good idea. I suggested that Jack sit in the cab because of leg problems and Hank can stay in back by himself. I fear that trying to disguise your presence could end up in revealing everything."

"Sure. I love riding in the cold wind," Hank said sardonically.

"You think we'll go by a checkpoint?" Jack asked.

"Highly probable," Monique answered. "We must not appear peculiar in any way. Talon can talk at the checkpoint if necessary and explain we're on the way to market. I can add anything else. I believe that's our best plan."

"You're the boss," Jack said. "You know better than we do."

"Okay." Monique pointed to the truck. "As soon as we're finished, Talon will start us on our way to Calais."

After breakfast, they straightened up the barn and got themselves ready. Talon kept racing the truck's motor as if he feared once it stopped, the vehicle would not start again. Finally, they piled in and Talon aimed the truck down the road. The flat top on the cab and the straight windshield made the square cab look more like an observation box on a road sign or a hunting blind. When they got on the highway, twenty-five miles an hour proved to be the top speed for the old Renault that no longer had springs, causing the bounce of the road to feel more like a blow from a sledge hammer.

Talon sat behind the wheel with a sparkle in his eye. The old man kept grinning and oversteering the truck. Driving a vehicle apparently fulfilled a long-hidden urge. The Renault chugged down the road, jerking back and forth across the highway and giving Jack constant concern.

The ride down the highway proved uneventful. Rolling countryside with dabs of snow here and there proved alluring and made Jack think of home in Texas where cows wandered around the pasture just as they did on the fields of Pas de Calais, even though the trees were far more abundant and the land not as flat. The slow speed of the truck made the vehicle feel like it might get to the town of Calais sometime next year. Eventually, they reached the turnoff from the main highway where the road veered toward the sea. A German checkpoint loomed on the road ahead of them. Three soldiers had the highway blocked and were waiting to examine their papers. The soldier who appeared to be in charge stood in the middle of the road with his hand raised.

"*Stoppen!*" the German demanded.

Talon pulled the truck to a stop and stuck his papers through the window.

The officer looked at them for a moment and then pointed to the others. "*Das anderers!*"

Talon shoved the papers of the other three through the window. The soldier walked around looking at each one carefully. Finally he handed the papers back and motioned for them to drive on. Jack looked over his shoulder and noticed the soldier writing something down on a notepad.

"Look!" Jack whispered. "The Kraut's taking notes."

Monique looked. "Not unusual. I wouldn't worry."

"Let's hope so." Jack turned back in his seat. "We don't need any problems."

Talon pointed straight ahead. "Calais."

Once they cleared the hill, Jack could see the tops of houses and the outlines of buildings. He smiled and nodded back to the old man. The ancient truck kept sputtering along.

Jack thought about what had happened on these very fields in other centuries. From time immemorial men had fought on this terrain with everything from stone knives to steel swords and spears. The Normans had ridden across the hills on horseback preparing to wage wars against the English. Napoleon had marched his armies up and down this countryside in arrogant defiance of the rest of Europe. On this day armored tanks and airplanes were poised to wipe out the opposition. Time had only improved the instruments of death, not alleviated the urge to kill. Had the centuries improved the character of humanity? Apparently not.

In a few minutes they would drive into this little French town where Jack hoped he would leave the country without having to fight another battle. Had this race to avoid death at the hands of the Nazis improved his character? Jack wasn't sure. He felt stripped of almost every other impulse except his survival instincts.

CHAPTER TWENTY-FOUR

*T*alon's old truck rumbled into the town of Calais. The edge of town looked like the average fishing village with small houses where locals lived. Houses appeared no larger than small cottages with nets stretched over the short fence lines. Bobbers and fishing rigs hung from nails at the corners of the houses. At some houses women stood outside by clotheslines, hanging up their washing. The villagers went about their business as if they were indifferent to the Nazi occupation.

They weren't.

German soldiers stood around on the street corners making casual conversation, but rifles hanging off their shoulders signaled intent. In a couple of blocks, Jack Martin saw enough of the *Wehrmacht* to make it clear that enough of them were hanging around the town that if they stumbled once the enemy would be on their backs before they had a chance to stand up. They would have to be more than cautious. They were so near to an escape and yet so, so far from home.

Talon slowed the truck to a crawl and pulled alongside a small restaurant. He spoke to Monique in French. She listened carefully then nodded and gestured for Jack to get out of the truck. Hank crawled out of the back.

"Talon is going to drive away now," Monique explained. "Don't look at him or make any gesture. He understands you appreciate his efforts, but the Germans may be watching. He will simply drive away and we will walk on as if we hitched a ride with him. That gives the trip a neutral appearance. We will go in to the café as if we are patrons. I'll do all the talking."

The two men nodded and followed the young French woman inside. A low ceiling with heavy, hand-planed beams made the room feel small and crowded. Men sat hunched over the tables drinking, talking quietly, and looking suspiciously at anyone who wandered in. Many, with heavy beards and thick woolen caps pulled down over their ears, looked like fishermen. The mix of locals appeared to be rough and ready. Jack and Hank found a table near the back wall and squeezed in. Monique walked to the front and talked to the man operating the café. Their conversation quickly became intense. After a few minutes she returned to the table with cups of coffee in her hands.

"The owner tells me the Nazis watch everything that happens in this town and expect the Allies to make some sort of penetration around here in the near future," Monique explained. "We must walk slowly, casually, and appear indifferent. We can sit in the café as long as we wish. No one will bother us."

"Do you think Talon got out okay?" Jack asked.

"He's in his eighties," Monique said. "An old man shouldn't be much of a threat to the Nazis. I would hope so."

Hank grinned. "He's a clever man. Talon will do all right."

"We may need to sit here for several hours," Monique said. "We won't attempt to find St. Pierre Street until the sun is lower in the sky. Time will have to pass before it's safe to approach house No. 8."

"No complaints from me," Hank said. "I can sit in here out of that cold wind for as long as you wish."

"Come on, tough guy," Jack said. "I thought you could withstand anything."

"Of course!" Hank grinned. "I just like this warm café a tad better than the freezing wind whistling down my neck."

"How are your legs?" Monique asked Jack.

"Better today. All the stretching helps make the skin more mobile. I guess you noticed that I left the crutches back at the barn."

Monique nodded.

"I figured they were too obvious. I've got to make it on my own no matter how painful it gets."

"I appreciate the thought, but I hope you don't have any problems," Monique said. "I doubt if you'd be able to do much in a fight."

"You don't mince words," Jack said. "I suppose I'm still below my usual standards. Don't worry. If we get into a showdown, I'll hold my own."

"Really?" Monique's eyes narrowed. "Let's hope we don't have to find out. Frankly, I doubt if you'd be able to get in more than one punch before the Nazis laid you out." She shook her finger in his face. "Don't be foolishly brave, Jack. You still limp, and even a woman can see your limitations."

Jack squirmed uncomfortably.

"Let me tell you Yanks something you must remember," Monique said. "We've found the Germans to be tough as leather boots. Some of 'em are just boys, but many of the infantry are strong, hard farm boys. They can be as vicious as guard dogs. Don't think you can toy with them and walk away. Particularly you, Jack! They didn't sweep through France in a few weeks because our soldiers were women." She lowered her voice. "Don't ever underestimate the adversary if you want to go on living another day."

No one said anything for a long time. Monique's "little talk" had a sobering effect. In the quiet, Jack realized that he had tended to slip into an attitude that underestimated the power of the enemy. Monique was correct. The Germans were a formidable adversary, and he was a recovering injured pilot with significant burns up and down his legs. The realization left him feeling weak and vulnerable, but the truth was Monique hit the nail on the head. If confronted, he wouldn't be of much use in the battle. In fact, Jack knew he was more of a deficit than anything else.

Thirty minutes later the front door opened and two German soldiers walked in. Instantly all talking stopped and everyone looked away. The soldiers glared around the room as if trying to decide whether to stay. Jack stared at the tabletop, doing everything possible to avoid making eye contact. The soldiers eventually turned and left as if the atmosphere had proved too inhospitable. Talking began again.

"Good boys," Monique said. "Keep that humble look on your face and you'll live longer."

"No problem," Hank said. "No problem at all."

Shortly past midafternoon the sun started lowering in the sky and throwing long shadows across the restaurant. Men had come and gone, but now fewer men filled the room. The fact that no one had spoken to them signaled something, but Jack wasn't sure what.

"Okay," Monique said. "I think the time has come for a leisurely stroll down the street. Walk as if you had all the time in the world."

"Oh yeah!" Jack said. "I won't have any trouble doing that."

"Get up and walk out without speaking to anyone," Monique said. "We're on our way."

Jack nodded. "Here we go." Feeling like a piece of wilted lettuce, he got up and tried not to limp, but even at his best Jack couldn't make his legs flexible. He hobbled out of the restaurant and started down the street.

They walked as if they were in no hurry to get anywhere. Just citizens coming and going from the ocean town. Monique looked like the other French women standing in front of the small shops. With their dull black hair, the two men seemed to be villagers or visitors to the harbor town . . . except for Jack's stiff-legged gait.

Once they cleared several blocks, the threesome came to a winding street that paralleled the Strait of Dover. A singular sign nailed to a pole identified the little thoroughfare as St. Pierre Street.

"Found it!" Jack beamed. "We're here. Start watching for a No. 8."

"No trouble doing that," Hank said. "I'm ready to find that good ole house and drop in for a visit as quickly as I can."

"Keep the slow pace," Monique warned. "We're not out of the hot water yet."

St. Pierre didn't look particularly different from any other street in town except the houses bordered the ocean. Heavy wooden piers punctuated with thick boards provided a walkway over the sea. The lapping waves underneath resounded through the cracks in the planks. Watching for the numbers on each house studiously, they kept walking.

"Look," Monique said. "I think that's the house. Two buildings ahead. Set over the sea."

"Yeah," Jack said. "Should be No. 8. Let's move it."

"Not too fast," Monique cautioned. "Keep the innocuous look on your faces."

Jack's steps picked up slightly. "Trying not to run." He grinned at Monique. "I've waited a long time to get here."

"Oh!" Monique stopped. "I don't see the red cloth on the door. Not a good sign."

Jack groaned. "Think we've got a problem?"

"Don't know. We don't have any choice. Just keep walking."

Hank leaned closer to Monique. "Maybe they've gone to the store. Went out. Something unimportant."

"Let's hope so." Monique shook her head. "I don't like this, but keep moving so we don't look suspicious."

Jack's pace slowed and his limp became more persistent. "Guess we'll amble down to the end of the pier and come back later. Maybe they'll return by then."

"We have no other alternative." Monique pointed straight ahead. "Keep moving."

When Jack walked past the house, he looked longingly at the door and hesitated, but he didn't stop. For the first time, the cold wind set in with a sharp bite. He kept walking.

"*Halten!*" a voice rang out behind them.

Jack stopped breathing. He turned slowly.

Three men had stepped out of the shadows between two of the houses across the street from No. 8. Pointing German Lugers, the men in thick leather overcoats leveled their pistols at the threesome.

"*Stoppen!*" the heavyset man in front demanded. He motioned with his Luger for them to raise their hands.

Jack held up his hands slowly. A terrible ominous feeling descended over him. They were caught!

"*Sprechen sie Deutsch?*" the fat man in front barked.

Jack looked back and forth at his friends. No one spoke. He was the only one with the capacity to speak German. He nodded his head. "*Ya.*"

"The SS has been looking for you," the German said with a smirk on his face. "If I am not mistaken, you were blown out of the sky over Maastrich. Right?"

Jack stiffened, but didn't answer.

The German took a few steps toward Jack while the other two men stayed in place with their guns aimed. "Hmm. Hair on the dark side. Looks somewhat disguised to me." He chuckled. "Did you think you could actually deceive us? You are speaking to SS Agent Arnwolf Mandel. An officer of the Third Reich. My diligence in pursuing you across Belgium and France has brought us here today." He turned to the small man standing next to him. "Well, Gerhard, we have caught our prey! The Reich remains invincible."

"Quite impressive, Arnwolf." Gerhard Hackett grinned. "A woman, two men, and one with a limp. Such an ensemble couldn't be hidden. What do you want to do with them?"

"We could take them back to your offices for interrogation," Mandel said. "A little pressure, a few twists, might make their tongues move faster. Particularly the woman."

"Yes. That is true."

"Or, we could shoot them out here on the docks as a warning to all the citizens of Calais not to aid these criminals when they come running across France," Mandel said.

"Shoot them?" Hackett looked surprised. "Now? But we wouldn't do that!"

Mandel turned with a cold look in his eyes. "And why not?"

"Out here on the pier?"

Mandel shrugged. "What counts is that we caught them. I think their bodies would be unimportant except as evidence of the chase."

The small man blinked several times. "I-I d-don't think we should kill them at this moment. O-out here in plain sight."

Mandel grinned and leveled his pistol at Jack's chest. "I always wanted to kill an American. I think today is a good time."

Jack Martin slowly lowered his hands. If he was to die on this French ocean pier, it would not be holding his hands above his head in terror. Everything he had learned throughout his entire life had taught him to endure and walk with a confidence that the Almighty God had a hand on his life. He would not cower before this Gestapo agent even though in a few seconds the man would kill him. Perhaps, the clock had run out and his time had come, but his death would follow with all the dignity he had left, displaying himself before the world with pride in himself and his country. Even with pain in his legs, he would stand as tall as he possibly could. Jack's heart pounded like a drum about to burst.

"*Stoppen!*" the German demanded again.

Jack turned his open palms toward the enemy to prove that he concealed nothing. No deception here.

"What are you doing?" Hank whispered. "They'll kill us."

Jack kept lowering his arms.

"You're going to die." Arnwolf Mandel sighted down the gun barrel.

At that moment the door to house No. 8 swung open. Wearing his brown trench coat and red scarf, Carlo Roche stepped out of the entrance. He fired once, hitting Arnwolf Mandel in the side of the head.

Gerhard Hackett whirled sideways and started firing back at the house. Instantly a gun battle exploded. The other Gestapo aide began firing at both the prisoners and whoever was shooting at them. Men in the windows of No. 8 blasted away. Bullets exploded in every direction. Pieces of wood flew into the air. Glass broke. Suddenly the aide slipped to his knees and slowly fell forward on his face. Hackett crumpled into a ball on the wooden pier; his gun dropped from his hand.

Jack stood shaking in the midst of the pile of bodies. The explosion had happened so quickly that he had not even moved. He kept blinking, but not really seeing anything. In front of him lay the three Germans sprawled across the pier.

Carlo Roche raced out of the doorway and stood over Mandel. Aiming at the German's chest, he fired one shot.

"Arabella Kersten sends her love!" Carlo growled. He motioned for Jack to get in the house. "Hurry up!" he said in English. "Get in here!"

Jack ran as fast as his legs would allow and leaped through the entrance. Some man grabbed him and pushed him against the wall. The man rattled off something in French, but Jack couldn't understand a word. Another man started slamming the windows shut. Jack's heart beat so hard that he could barely breathe. Slumping against the wall, he glanced around the house, trying to orient himself. It looked like a two- or three-room bungalow.

"Hank?" Jack said. "Where's Hank?" He glanced around the room. Nobody seemed to understand him. Grabbing the curtain, he pulled it back and peered out. Jack froze in place. "God, help us!" he groaned.

Hank Holt lay on his back with his arms and legs extended like branches on a fallen tree. His body didn't seem bent or twisted by violence, but his empty eyes were wide open, staring up into the vast sky above him. A single hole in the middle of his forehead told the rest of the story.

Jack jerked backwards. For a moment his heart stopped and his knees buckled. A wave of nausea swept over him. Thinking he misunderstood, Jack looked a second time, but there was no misinterpretation. His best friend in the world was dead. Tears stormed into Jack's eyes.

"Stop it!" Monique screamed in his ears. "Soldiers will be here in a moment. We must hide!"

Jack couldn't speak and wasn't sure he could move.

Monique yanked his shirt violently. "Listen to me! We've got to run. Follow me!"

A wooden door swung open in the center of the floor and Monique immediately started down a makeshift ladder. Some man pushed Jack hard and he mechanically dropped through the hole. His feet took on a life of their own. The violent pounding of his heart seemed to push the agony in his legs aside. He scampered down the wooden steps and dropped into a small boat. Before he knew what happened, the boat jerked forward and he fell on his back on top of the ribs of the boat. The pain shook him.

"Don't move!" Monique shouted in his face. "Just lie there."

The cold water of the ocean had seeped in from somewhere and sent a chill down his body. Underneath his coat, Jack's shirt instantly became wet. He felt like a helpless child floundering around on the floor after trying to take his first step. Helplessness, terror, panic merged into a deadly mix contaminating his mind.

Monique whispered something in French. The two men steering the boat nodded and one man pointed straight ahead down to the end of the pier. The boat kept gliding through the ocean and hovering beneath the houses and pier above them. In a few minutes the craft had made it down the length of the village. All that was left was the open water before them. One of the men reached over the edge and tied the boat to the end of a large landing built out into the channel. The other man pulled a tarp over all of them.

"Lie flat and don't move!" Monique demanded. "We've got to wait for it to get a bit darker before we set out into the sea. Don't move. The Nazis will be all over the piers."

Jack lay in the cold water jostling around under his body.

He wanted to move, but knew better. No matter what his cold skin tried to tell him, he couldn't listen. In the darkness under the tarp, he suddenly realized Monique was crouched next to him, only inches from his face. He could feel her warm breath.

"They'll think Hank and the Gestapo agents had a battle when they tried to arrest him," Monique whispered. "Probably assume anyone with them got away. The townspeople would protect anybody fleeing the Nazis and the Germans know it. They'll run everybody into the center of the village to scare them and that's when we'll slip away."

Jack nodded but didn't answer. In this black hole he once again felt frighteningly alone. Every step of the path had been filled with death. And now he had a new question that left him as terrified as any of the others. Why Hank and not him?

Jack felt ashamed and humiliated. Hank had saved him twice, and Jack had not even begun to return anything for his friend's valor. Jack wanted to curl up in a ball and die. He had experienced the deaths of Dirk Vogel, Madame Somerville, Burnell Manville, the Etienne brothers, and now Hank. How could he explain such self-sacrifice to anyone? The truth was that he couldn't. In the dark, tears trickled down his cheeks. All he could do was thank God for the life of Hank Holt and commit his friend to the care of the Almighty. Once more he prayed the same intercession for the others. In the dark silence underneath the tarp, Jack felt like he was the last soldier left in the world. He had no idea how long he'd been there when Monique spoke again.

"Listen!" the French woman abruptly said. "Do you hear it?"

"Sounds like an Allied bomber," Jack said. "Maybe bombers. Coming this way."

"Yes." Monique squirmed. "Don't like it. Don't like it at all."

The roar of the airplanes increased. From somewhere the sound of canons shooting at the sky filled the air. Off in the distance, exploding bombs shook the earth.

The two Frenchmen quickly became animated and started speaking rapidly to Monique. Whipping back the tarp, they untied the boat and pushed out into the water. When Jack looked back at Calais, he saw the lights of the entire town were turned off. The air raid had sent the village into retreat and darkness. Obviously, this was the right moment to launch into the English Channel. The men heaved at the oars, pushing away from the coast of France as fast as they could. Within a few minutes the shoreline disappeared and all he could see in front of him was a vast waterway.

Monique huddled next to him. "I know you're wet," she said. "Unfortunately, we don't have anything extra for you to put on. You'll have to hang on."

"I'm okay," Jack said. "Better off than Hank."

"Don't think about what happened back there," Monique warned. "I've told you before. You can't let yourself dwell on what occurred. It'll kill you."

Jack nodded. "How well I understand." He lowered his head and stared at the bottom of the boat.

"I want you to know that we consider it an honor to have helped in this struggle to set you free," Monique said. "It's one of the important ways we can fight the Germans. If we save one American, we've sent a warrior back into the battle against this insidious evil. You must not think about those who have fallen. They gave their lives gladly because there's no higher service to be rendered in this war. Laying themselves down to die is the highest honor possible. There is no greater love."

Jack listened. Her words weren't hollow, but at this moment he couldn't quite grasp what she was saying. Too much had happened too quickly. He kept looking out into the dark night. The bitter cold winter swept over him and the waves lapped up against the side of the boat. The Frenchmen kept rowing and the little boat sailed on toward England.

"Jack!" Monique said. "Hang on. Jack, you'll make it."

Jack stared into the black night.

"Jack, do you hear me?"

EPILOGUE

*J*ack? Do you hear me?"

Martin blinked several times. He'd heard his wife's voice a million times. For some reason she sounded different tonight.

"Jack! You've been out here in the backyard for nearly an hour. It's getting late!"

Jack Martin looked toward his house. At that moment Dallas, Texas, seemed different. Everything seemed different. He had to touch the fence to make sure he was standing in his own backyard. Nothing felt right. Even the fence looked different.

"Are you listening to me?" Martha sounded irritated. "I want you to come in. It's getting close to bedtime."

"Just a moment!" Jack shouted back. "Yes, I'm coming in."

He had stepped back across six decades as if his story had unfolded yesterday morning. Well, in fact, the whole episode seemed more vibrant than whatever had happened the day before. Jack was surprised how fresh each memory seemed.

Hank Holt couldn't be dead! Could he? Of course he was, but it didn't seem like sixty years since he had fallen on that pier. Sixty years ago? Jack shuddered. It was true. This valiant friend had fallen a long time ago, but even now Jack had to fight the tears back. The memory remained too painful. Jack wiped his eyes.

During the past decades he had often wondered what had become of Monique Sernin. She had simply vanished in the night as had Carlo Roche, and so many others. Their faces remained only in his memory. Maybe they had survived the war; maybe they hadn't. He could only pray they were still alive somewhere in France, even today. Happy old people comforted by their memories of service to their country and mankind. All of them had been special friends whether he knew them for a long time or not. Voices like Reverend Harold Assink or Dirk Vogel had disappeared from his mind, but the themes they stood for remained tried and true. He knew that the British, American, and Belgian governments had honored Julien and Ann Brusselman. Jack could only wish that people like Burnell Manville and the Etienne brothers had received the same. What courage they had! The world could certainly use more of their kind. He'd put his own medals away and never spoke of the Silver Star and the Purple Heart the military had given him. Didn't seem right in light of what all those other people did. He'd never told Martha about any of those things that happened before they met.

"Jack," Martha said. "Are you all right? You've been out in this cold weather for a long time."

Jack turned and looked at his wife. "Cold? Not really."

"Not really!" Martha protested. "It might even frost to-night!"

Jack nodded. "I've lived through days when I thought I'd freeze to death. Just don't talk about them."

Martha frowned. "I have no idea what you are talking about." She looked at him thoughtfully. "I think that call from Maastrich upset you, dear. You never talk about the war. Is that what this is all about?"

Jack looked away. She was right. He'd avoided the subject of the war at all costs. The pain of remembering people who died to save others was too difficult, but Jack knew he should talk about it. He needed to tell her, the children, bring it out in the open. It had been way too long, but now the right time had come.

He turned slowly and looked Martha squarely in the eye. Jack felt his lip tremble slightly and had to clear his throat. Martha was looking back at him almost as if she were afraid of what he might say. Her tendency to take charge of things had disappeared and concern filled her eyes.

"Jack, are you okay?"

"Yes." He pointed toward his legs. "You know those scars on my legs? I never really told you the story, the whole story. I think I've waited far too long. I want you to know what happened to me during the war."

"Oh, my dear!" Martha hugged him. "I've always wanted to understand." She shook her head. "I knew it was bad. You wouldn't talk about it, you know." Martha touched his cheek. "If you want to tell me, I'd so like to hear all about it. I'm in no hurry. We can talk as long as you wish."

Jack put his arm around her shoulder and started walking back to the house. "We'll need to sit down because it will take me awhile to talk it out. You've never heard me speak of my old friend Hank Holt or of the Brusselmans . . . or Monique Sernin. I want you to know about a young Dutch boy named Dirk Vogel. Wonderful people." He had to stop and bite his lip.

"Yes," Martha said. "All new names to me." She squeezed his hand.

"It began in the fall when the weather was cold like tonight. My airplane was shot down by the Germans." He stopped. "Hard to talk about. Most of my men disappeared." Jack took a few more steps. "Certainly hard to talk about."

"I understand," Martha said. "Take your time."

Jack opened the back door and followed Martha into the kitchen. He sat down at the kitchen table and she waited across from him. "I never knew how loving friends could be," he began. "How very, very good people are . . ."

More Great Reads from Robert Wise!

ISBN 0-8054-3072-5
$12.99

Historical fiction based on the true story of Allied prisoners in World War II held near the German border in the medieval castle known as Colditz.

ISBN 0-8054-3073-3
$12.99

A clergyman comes face-to-face with man's inhumanity to man in the Dachau concentration camp, forcing him to ask tough questions about God that ultimately propel him into a fresh understanding of life itself.

"Wise knows how to deliver suspense," says Booklist.

Look for his novels at bookstores nationwide or visit www.broadmanholman.com today!

BROADMAN
& HOLMAN
PUBLISHERS